Fascism Speaks
Book 1

Also from EATMS Productions

Nonfiction
Billionaires, Capitalism, and Power

Evil and the Mountain Ungreed
Self Help for American Billionaires
Selfish Steve and the Ivory Tower
Tariffs, Taxes, & Face-Eating Leopards
Ban Billionaires: Fascism Fix

Fascism, Religion, and Cultural Control

Self Help for the Manosphere
Fascism 2025
Fascism & the Perverts & the Greed Virus
Christian Fascism Marriage Book
Tyranny, Table Manners, & Tiramisu

Guides for Women's Autonomy and Protection

How to Survive in Post-America as a Woman
Project 2025 American Drag
4B – Burn, Ban, Boycott, Build
4B OG – So No Go GYN
I'm Glad He's Dead

Analysis of Authoritarian Project 2025

Project 2025: The Blueprint
Project 2025: The List
Project 2025, Christian Dumb Dumbs, & The Republican Agenda
Fascism, Project 2025, & The Pinkprint

Modern Rewrites for Women

Stoic Principles Reimagined
Siddhartha Reimagined
The Prince Reimagined for Women
The Art of War Reimagined for Women
The Jungle Reimagined
The Constitution Reimagined for Women

Machine Learning Series

AI, Bitcoin, Nostr for Women
AI, Safety, & Security for Women
AI, Anxiety, & Health for Women
AI, Kids, & Family Safety for Women
AI, Creativity, & Personal Expression for Women
AI, Independent Work, & Parallel Power for Women

Social Systems Series

Emotional Labor for Women
Household Power for Women
Workplace Power for Women
Medical Bias for Women
Aging Systems for Women
Recovery Systems for Women

Fiction
Propaganda Paige & the Missing Prosperity
Propaganda Paige & the TIDE Manifesto
Propaganda Paige & the Shadow Cartographers
Propaganda Paige & the Prosperity Alliance
Propaganda Paige & the Shattered Truth
Propaganda Paige & the Rising TIDE
Propaganda Paige & the Last Bastion
Propaganda Paige & the Dawn of Prosperity
Project 2025: Dorian — The Last Men
Project 2025: Boy — A Last Men Novel

Propaganda Paige & The Missing Prosperity

Fascism Speaks 1/8

by
Sable Moncrieff

EATMS
P R O D U C T I O N S

ISBN: 978-1-966014-19-5

Cover, interior design by: Esme Mees

eatms@pm.me
www.eatms.me

Check out EATMS Underground:
https://tinyurl.com/eatmsNOSTR

Printed in the United States of America.

If particular care and attention is not paid to the ladies, we are determined to foment a rebellion, and will not hold ourselves bound to any laws in which we have no voice or representation.

— Abigail Adams

Table of Contents

Foreword

They told you history was written by great men. They told you prosperity was their gift to the world. That's a lie. Every empire, every revolution, every parchment promise was inked in blood that wasn't theirs. Paige isn't here to remember them. She's here to erase them.

This isn't the story of liberty. It's the story of payback. No more statues, no more marble myths. Only the sound of bones breaking, of wigs catching fire, of prosperity rotting where it began. The Fathers built a world on stolen backs. Paige is the correction.

—Esme Mees, Summer 2025

~1
Enter Philadelphia

Philadelphia, 1776. The city smells like rot, horses, shit, and smoke. The streets are mud and piss. Pigs root through garbage. Rats scatter from cart wheels. Independence Hall looms at the center like a proud tumor. The land where prosperity was said to be born.

Inside that hall, men talk about freedom. Outside, they sell it.

Paige lands in the filth of an alley, knees bending, boots sinking ankle-deep in slime. She doesn't fall; she never does. The fold spits her out as if history itself is sick of carrying her. She adjusts the strap across her chest. Knife in sheath, pistol tucked, powder horn rattling with each step. She smells the city: sweat, wood smoke, iron, and blood.

The crowd's noise pulls her like a current. Male voices raised in laughter, money exchanged in loud declarations. Then the crack of a whip. A woman screaming. Paige moves.

It's a slave auction.

A platform, rough-hewn wood, raised above the mud. Torches bracket it, flames whipping in the summer air. A dozen men in wigs and coats stand in the front row, brandy in hand. Behind them: farmers, sailors, boys too young to grow beards. And at the center of the stage: a girl, no older than thirteen. Her wrists bound, dress torn at the collar, bare feet caked in mud. She stares down at nothing.

The auctioneer is a fat man with pockmarked cheeks, red nose, powdered wig askew. He grins, raising her arm as if she's game at the end of a hunt. His whip cracks again, close enough to her back to make her flinch. The crowd roars with laughter.

"Fine little piece," he bellows. "Strong hips. Good for work, good for bed. Who'll start me at fifty?"

Coins clink. Voices shout numbers. The girl closes her eyes.

Paige doesn't climb up yet. She watches. She listens. The men call out bids like they're at a horse fair. One pinches his friend's arm and laughs, "She's worth double if she keeps her mouth shut." Another sloshes his brandy, shouting "Sixty! Sixty for the little whore!"

And in the front row, three men stand like monuments.

Benjamin Franklin, his jowls slack from too much drink, grins through his spectacles. He whispers to a friend about "breeding value."

John Adams, squat and severe, frowns, as if the auction is distasteful only because it looks chaotic. He doesn't leave.

Thomas Jefferson, fox-eyed, scribbles in a leather-bound notebook, recording prices with the cool detachment of a man cataloguing cattle.

Paige fixes them in her sight. The names she's heard whispered in classrooms, printed on coins, carved in marble. Here they are, in flesh, drinking and watching while a child is sold.

The whip cracks again. The girl flinches, shoulders twitching.

That's enough.

Paige steps forward. She moves through the crowd. A man in a blue coat blocks her path, smirking. "Not your place, bitch." He jabs his cane at her chest.

She smashes her elbow into his face. Cartilage snaps. He screams as blood gushes down his chin. He collapses into the mud, clutching his ruined nose.

Heads turn. The laughter falters. Franklin lowers his brandy. Jefferson's quill stills. Adams scowls deeper.

Paige keeps walking. She climbs the steps to the platform. The girl stares at her, wide-eyed, confused. The auctioneer blinks in disbelief.

"What's this?" he sneers. "Another buyer? Or just another whore sniffing for work?"

He cracks the whip at her face.

Paige catches it mid-air. The crowd gasps.

She yanks. The leather coils around his wrist. He tries to pull back, but she jerks hard. The whip tightens like a snake. Bones snap. Skin tears. His hand rips clean off, spraying blood across the stage and onto the bidders below.

The girl screams.

The auctioneer drops to his knees, staring dumbly at the stump gushing blood. His severed hand lies twitching in the mud.

Paige pulls her knife. Steel gleams in the torchlight.

A bidder leaps onto the stage, cane raised like a club. Paige slashes his throat. Blood fans across the girl's legs, painting her skin red. The man staggers, gargling, and collapses twitching at her feet.

Another man draws a pistol. Paige hurls the knife. It slams into his eye with a wet crunch. He topples backward, convulsing, pistol clattering useless to the boards.

The crowd screams. Panic erupts.

Some surge toward the stage, others scramble over each other to flee.

The auctioneer whimpers, clutching his stump. "Help me! God help me!"

Paige yanks his wig, hauls him upright. "God's busy."
She slams his face into the podium. Wood cracks. Teeth
scatter like dice across the boards. She slams him again,
harder. His skull bursts. Brains spray across the ledger
where he kept his accounts.

The girl is frozen, shaking. Paige slices the rope around
her wrists. "Run."

The girl doesn't move. Paige shoves her hard. "Go!"

She stumbles off the stage into the arms of women at
the edge, washerwomen, widows, prostitutes. They pull
her close, shielding her, staring at Paige like she's death
itself.

A bidder trips in the mud, scrambling away. Paige leaps
down after him. She stomps on his spine. It cracks. He
screams once, then goes limp.

Another crawls on elbows, leaving a red smear. Paige
rips his wig off and shoves it into his mouth. He
thrashes, gagging. She pushes harder until he chokes,
his eyes bulging, face turning purple.

A boy, sixteen, maybe, stares at her, pistol shaking in
his hands. "Please."

Paige rips it away, jams the barrel under his chin, and
pulls the trigger. His head bursts in a spray of bone and
brain. "Grow up in hell."

The crowd collapses into chaos. Men run screaming.
The women hold the freed girl tighter.

Franklin watches, pale now, brandy forgotten. Adams mutters curses, tugging his sleeve. Jefferson closes his notebook, slips it into his coat, and retreats into shadow, his fox grin lingering.

Paige wipes her knife on a dead man's coat. She spits on the auctioneer's body.

"Prosperity, my ass."

She turns and walks toward Independence Hall.
The square was a graveyard. Torches hissed in the humid air, light catching the blood pooling in the mud. Bodies lay twisted on the ground, wigs half-submerged, faces slack, eyes staring up at nothing. The stink of piss and powder clung to everything.

The survivors hadn't left. They lingered at the edges: behind overturned carts, in tavern doorways, peeking out from alley mouths. Not one of them dared move closer to the stage, but not one of them could look away.

They whispered.

Witch.
Devil.
Judgment.

Paige didn't flinch. She walked among the corpses, pulling her knife free from a bidder's eye socket, wiping the steel clean on his embroidered coat. She crouched, picked up a pistol from the boy she'd blown apart. Checked powder, cocked it, slid it into her belt.

Efficient, quiet, like someone packing tools after a day's work.

The women still huddled at the edge with the freed girl pressed tight against them. One woman, gray-haired and wide-eyed, finally spoke, voice breaking: "What are you?"

Paige looked at them for a beat. The girl's face was blank, all the tears already burned out of her. Paige's answer was flat, as cold as her blade.

"Not your savior. Just your propaganda."

Gasps. A few women crossed themselves. None stepped forward. A drunk lurched from a nearby tavern, confused by the silence. He blinked at the carnage, stumbled closer, and shrieked. He turned to run, but Paige grabbed him by the collar and yanked him back. He whimpered, squirming in her grip.

"You laughed when the whip cracked," she said loud enough for the whole square to hear. She slammed his face into the stage. "You cheered when they priced her like a pig." She shoved his head into the blood pooled at the base of the platform. He thrashed, bubbling, choking. She pressed until his body went slack. She let him fall face-down in the muck, drowned in the blood of men he'd called brothers.

The whispering swelled. *Witch. Executioner. Wrath.*

A sailor tried to slip away down a side alley. Paige didn't even turn her head when she raised the pistol.

One sharp crack, his skull burst against the wall, body crumpling in a twitching heap. The crowd shrieked and shrank back. Good. They would remember.

Paige scanned the shadows. Franklin was gone from the front, but she caught a glimpse of him retreating into the alley, coat flapping, face pale as chalk. Adams's voice carried, sharp and furious: "We'll root her out! Mark me, she won't last!" He sounded less like a leader, more like a cornered rat. Jefferson was nowhere to be seen. But she knew his type, quiet, writing, watching. He'd be plotting in ink even as he fled.

She adjusted her knife, reloaded the pistol, and kept walking.

The tavern across the square was lit with lamplight. Inside, men huddled around a table, muskets stacked against the wall. Soldiers, local militia. They'd been drinking while the auction went on. Now they sat frozen, staring through the glass at her like children who'd seen the boogeyman step into their house.

Paige kicked the door open. Wood splintered. The men leapt to their feet. One lunged for a musket. Paige shot him in the chest. He toppled backward into the table, sending mugs and coins flying.

Another fumbled for powder. She flipped the table with her boot. It crashed against the wall, ale flooding the floor. She slashed the next man across the jaw. His face split from cheek to ear. He screamed, blood spraying across the lamplight. She shoved her knife through his throat and yanked it free. He collapsed gurgling.

The others broke. Two ran for the door. Paige grabbed a lantern and hurled it. Flames raced across the ale-soaked boards. The men shrieked as fire crawled up their legs. One tried to beat the flames with his coat, screaming until his voice cut off in a choking howl.

A single soldier dropped his musket and raised his hands. "Please. Mercy."

Paige leveled the pistol at his face. "Freedom," she said, and pulled the trigger. His head snapped back, blood spraying across the burning wall. The tavern roared with fire. Paige stepped outside as smoke billowed, leaving the soldiers to burn.

The square was nearly empty now. Only the women remained, clutching the freed girl like she was their last candle in the dark. They watched Paige step through the smoke and ash, watched her pass by without a word. At the far end of the street, Independence Hall glowed. Shadows flickered in its tall windows, the congressmen still inside, drafting their so-called liberty. Paige spat into the mud. "Let's see what liberty really costs."

She walked toward the hall, boots sticky with blood, knife still dripping. Behind her, the whispers followed like a tide:
Witch.
Demon.
Reckoning.

And then the square was empty, save for the corpses cooling in the torchlight

~2
The Scribes

The chamber reeked of sweat, ink, and stale pipe smoke. Heavy curtains blocked out most of the Philadelphia sunlight, leaving the air thick and hot. Men shifted in their chairs, mopping their powdered faces, tugging at collars that seemed suddenly too tight. The smell of damp wool and unwashed flesh hung over the room.

Paige sat near the back at a long table, hunched over parchment like every other "scribe." A blotch of ink stained her fingers. Her head was lowered, eyes flicking upward just enough to watch them through her lashes. She looked like another quiet clerk, a shadow with no voice. Nobody noticed the knife strapped to her calf or the steady rhythm of her breathing.

At the front of the room, Thomas Jefferson stood with a quill in hand, pacing as he dictated. His voice had a preacher's cadence, rising and falling, meant to sound like scripture.

"We hold these truths to be self-evident…" he began, letting the words hang in the stale air. His colleagues leaned in, some nodding gravely, others smirking. Franklin whispered something that made Adams bark a sharp laugh.

Paige's jaw clenched. She wrote the words onto her own scrap of parchment with a slow hand, the letters crawling like a disease across the page.

Jefferson continued, "...that all men are created equal."

Paige whispered it under her breath, flat and cold: *"Not anymore."*

No one heard.

The room was a theater, and these men were actors playing at divinity. They congratulated each other with nods and chuckles, trading lines like they were rewriting the Bible itself. Outside, Paige knew, enslaved children ran errands through mud. Women stitched their coats, cooked their food, wiped their asses, and had no seat in this chamber. Inside, the men pretended they were birthing freedom.

Adams slammed his fist on the table. "We must be clear! Liberty does not mean license. The people must have order." His voice rattled the wood panels.

Jefferson gave a lazy nod, dipping his quill into ink. Franklin smirked, muttering something to a delegate beside him. The two chuckled like schoolboys in a pew.

Paige dipped her own pen. Ink blotted, staining her fingertips black. Her pulse throbbed in her ears.

The rhythm of the room was almost hypnotic, scrape of chairs, shuffle of papers, Jefferson's voice riding above it all. She watched their lips move, heard the scratch of their quills. The hypocrisy was a symphony, and she sat silent at the back, waiting for the perfect note to cut it in two.

Jefferson raised his voice. "…that among these are life, liberty, and the pursuit of happiness." He said it like he believed it.

Paige's hand tightened around her pen. She imagined driving it through his throat. She imagined the sound of cartilage splitting, blood spilling over his papers. Not yet. Too soon.

The doors creaked open briefly as a servant carried in a tray of brandy and glasses. The men paused to drink, to wet their lips before resuming their holy work. The servant, a thin young woman with eyes cast to the floor, did not exist to them. She moved among the tables like furniture, silent and ignored.

Paige's eyes followed her. She thought of the auctioneer's hand spurting blood in the square. She thought of the girl she freed.

Not your savior. Just your propaganda.

The girl's stare still clung to her.

The brandy glasses clinked. Adams laughed too loud. Franklin wiped sweat from his brow and tugged at his wig. Jefferson returned to his pacing.

Paige copied every word onto her parchment, slow and deliberate. Ink smeared across her hand. The blotches looked like bruises. She wrote until her page swam in front of her eyes, the letters crawling. She whispered each line to herself like a curse.

"All men are created equal." Her lips twisted. "Governments are instituted among men." Her hand tightened. "Deriving their just powers from the consent of the governed." Her breath hissed.

Her eyes flicked up. Jefferson was close now, pacing past her table. He held his own quill like a priest holds a cross. His free hand brushed against the desk in front of her.

He didn't see her eyes. If he had, he might have stopped.

Paige's heartbeat slowed. The room blurred into muffled noise, Franklin's chuckle, Adams's rant, the scratch of quills. She heard only the whisper in her skull: *Do it now.*

She dipped her pen again. Ink pooled on the tip. She rolled it between her fingers, careful, slow. The men droned on. The weight of history pressed down on the room, and Paige's hand twitched.

She leaned forward, copying another line.

Her lips barely moved: *"…Not anymore."*

The words disappeared under the scratch of quills and the drone of Jefferson's voice.

Paige's hand tightened around the pen until her knuckles whitened. She could feel the sharp end trembling in her grip, hungry.

One more line. One more word.

She let her pen hover above the parchment. The chamber buzzed with pomp and heat. Sweat rolled down Jefferson's temple as he raised his hand for silence. The other delegates quieted, eyes on him. He dipped his quill in the inkpot, twirled it, and pressed the nib to fresh parchment.

"We hold these truths…" he began again, voice solemn.

Paige's grip tightened. Her pen trembled above her own page. She wasn't writing anymore. She was waiting.

Jefferson leaned over his desk, steadying the paper with one pale hand. His fingers spread across the wood, tapping lightly as he dictated. He looked out over the chamber like he was delivering divine revelation, a prophet of liberty.

Paige rose from her seat, slow enough that no one noticed at first. Her ink-stained hand slid across the table.

Jefferson turned his head slightly, catching her movement in the corner of his eye. His words faltered.

"…to be self-evident."

She drove the quill straight through the back of his hand. The sound was a wet crunch, cartilage giving way as the nib split skin and dug into wood. Jefferson screamed, high-pitched, not dignified at all. His powdered wig tilted sideways as he thrashed. Blood geysered across the parchment, blooming red into the sacred words. The chamber erupted.

Adams shot to his feet, bellowing: "Seize her!" His face turned crimson, spittle flying from his lips.

Franklin ducked under the table, moving with surprising speed for his age. Other delegates stumbled backward, chairs clattering to the floor.

Paige leaned over Jefferson's desk, staring down at him as he clawed at the quill pinning his hand. His face contorted, eyes wide with disbelief. He looked like a child caught in a trap.

She hissed, low enough that only he could hear: "Not anymore."

Then she yanked the quill free. Blood poured down his arm, dripping off the edge of the desk. He howled, clutching his ruined hand to his chest. Ink splattered with the blood, staining his vest, his face, his parchment.

The delegates shouted over each other. One man drew a pistol with shaking hands. Paige snatched an inkpot from the table and hurled it at him. Glass shattered against his forehead, black ink mixing with blood as he tumbled backward.

Smoke filled the air as a lantern toppled, flames licking up the parchment. The words "Declaration" blurred and curled in the fire.

Paige stepped back, quill dripping red in her hand. She looked at the room of frightened men, patriots, philosophers, fathers of a nation. They cowered, screamed, scrambled.

One reached for her. She slashed his cheek open with the quill, the nib carving a jagged red line down his face. Another tried to bar the door. She kicked him in the chest, sending him crashing into the wood hard enough to splinter it.

Adams was still shouting, his voice cracking. "Devil woman! Witch! She'll damn us all!"

Paige turned her gaze on him, and he froze. His lips quivered, but the words stuck in his throat. He looked small, suddenly.

The flames spread fast. Papers curled, chairs caught. Men coughed and stumbled, trampling each other in their desperation to escape. A musket fired wildly, the ball lodging into the ceiling beam. Splinters rained down.

Franklin crawled out from under the table, coughing, his spectacles gone. He tried to shout something, a warning, a rally, but his voice vanished under the roar of fire.

Jefferson, still clutching his bleeding hand, dragged himself toward the far wall, leaving a crimson smear across the floorboards. His mouth opened and closed like a fish gulping for air. No words came.

Paige strode through the chaos, calm, steady. She shoved aside a panicked delegate, sidestepped another. She moved like a blade through cloth, cutting but untouched.

Behind her, the Declaration itself curled in the flames, words disappearing into smoke. The sacred paper shriveled, blackening at the edges until it fell apart into ash. The "birth" of a nation dissolved into fire and blood.

She reached the doors, paused, and looked back once more. The room was an inferno of smoke, panic, and history burning alive.

At the door, she turned back once. Jefferson was on his knees, clutching his bleeding hand, shrieking for help as smoke swirled around him. Franklin crawled on all fours toward an open window, wig half-burned, his face blackened with soot.

Paige held up the quill, slick with blood and ink.

"Let's see what you print now," she said.

Then she walked out.

The street outside was already alive with whispers. People craned their necks toward the hall, hearing the chaos within. A crowd gathered, women with baskets, workers in aprons, children peeking from behind skirts. Their eyes fixed on her as she emerged, blood on her hands, the quill gleaming in the sun.

Gasps rippled. Someone whispered, "She struck Jefferson." Another muttered, "She bled their words."

Paige tucked the quill into her belt, ink dripping down her thigh. She didn't stop walking.

Behind her, the hall filled with smoke. Shouts turned to screams, glass shattered. The crowd backed away from the doors as men tumbled out, coughing, faces streaked with soot and blood.

"Witch!" one of them shouted, pointing at her. "Seize her!"

But no one moved. The word hung in the air, heavy, poisonous, but powerless. The crowd only stared, eyes wide, breath held, torn between fear and awe.

An old woman near the front whispered, "Maybe she's not a witch. Maybe she's ours." A boy clutched her sleeve, staring at Paige as if she were a story stepping out of fire.

Paige kept walking. Her boots struck the cobblestones, steady, unhurried. The noise of the city seemed to hush around her, as though the streets themselves bent to listen.

At the corner, she paused. A young servant girl stood in the shadows, clutching an empty pitcher. Her eyes locked on Paige's. No fear, no awe, just a hollow stare, like the freed girl from the auction.

Paige met her gaze for a long moment. Neither spoke. The silence between them was louder than the crowd's whispers.

Then Paige turned and disappeared into the warren of alleys, leaving smoke and rumors behind her. The crowd kept staring at the corner she'd vanished into, as if she might step back out, or never have been there at all.

~3
The Printing Press Massacre

The print shop at the end of Market Street looked asleep. The shutters were drawn tight, the lamps snuffed out, and only the faint smell of ink and hot iron clung to the humid night air. Inside, the press itself loomed like some enormous sleeping animal. The heavy oak beams groaned as they settled, the iron screws still ticked as they cooled, and the air hung thick with the sour tang of grease. Damp pages swayed on clotheslines strung across the rafters, thousands of them, the words *liberty* and *freedom* and *consent of the governed* fluttering above her head like a taunt.

Paige slipped in through a side door left carelessly unlatched, and the sound of her boots on the floorboards was no louder than the sigh of a mouse. She moved slowly, letting her eyes adjust to the dimness. The place had the quiet of a crypt, broken only by the occasional creak of the wood.

She ran her hand along the frame of the press. The oak was worn smooth where apprentices had gripped it with inky hands. She crouched low and studied the gears, the heavy rollers, the teeth that chewed paper into neat columns of words. She knew machines, how they worked, how they broke, how to make them turn against their masters. She pulled a short length of chain and a fistful of nails from the pouch at her hip and began working them into the rollers with the kind of precision you give a bomb. The iron teeth clinked softly as she fed the chain in, each sound amplified by the silence around her.

When the sabotage was set, she straightened, flexing her fingers. They were smeared black with ink and grease. She looked up at the damp pages swaying overhead and pulled one down. It was a broadside full of Franklin's pomp: *We are a people born free, united under Providence.* Paige crumpled it into a tight ball, shoved it in her mouth, and chewed until the pulp bled ink on her tongue. She spat the bitter wad onto the floorboards.

The press was silent now, waiting. She thought of Franklin, his sly wit, his twinkle, the old fox grin he wore like a mask. This was his temple, his pulpit, his altar. Every sheet printed here was a sermon to keep the people docile. She was going to make sure it choked on its own gospel.

Then the door creaked. Paige froze.

A pair of voices drifted in from the alley, low and complaining. "He wants another batch tonight? Christ, let him haul his own ass down here."

"Shut it. He's paying us, isn't he? You want to eat, you print."

Two boys stumbled in, arms loaded with paper. They weren't men yet, faces smooth, movements clumsy with fatigue. They dumped the reams on the workbench with a dusty thud, then one of them lit a lantern. The glow spilled across the room, landing on the gears where Paige had left her sabotage.

The younger one leaned in, squinting. "What the hell is that?"

The second crouched to get a closer look. His hand reached toward the chain knotted through the teeth. "Something's jammed in here."

Paige slid deeper into the shadows behind a tower of paper bundles. Her breath slowed. Her fingers rested on the hilt of her knife.

The boys rattled the chain nervously, tugged at the nails, and then froze. One whispered the word like a prayer, like a curse: "The witch."

The silence that followed was heavy. Paige could hear her own pulse.

The door opened again. Heavier steps this time, more certain. An older apprentice entered, shoulders broad, face smudged with ink. He took one look at the jammed press and snarled. "Sabotage."

The two younger boys flinched. One stammered, "It's her. It has to be her."

The older one glared around the room, nostrils flaring. He grabbed the lantern from the table and held it high, sweeping its light across the shadows.

The glow slid closer to Paige's hiding place. She pressed herself against the wall, unmoving. The light skimmed across the floor and stopped at her boot. The boy's eyes widened.

Paige rose slowly, stepping from the shadows with the knife in her hand. She didn't lunge. She didn't speak. She simply let them see her, the blood-stained ink on her fingers, the cold gleam in her eyes.

The younger apprentices gasped and stepped back. The older one stood his ground, though his jaw clenched tight.

For a long moment, none of them moved. The press loomed behind them, the chain groaning faintly in its gears, as if it were alive and waiting.

The older boy's voice cracked when he spoke. "Run."

The others didn't need telling twice. They bolted through the door, papers scattering in their wake, their footsteps echoing down the lane.

Only Paige and the older one remained. The lantern flickered between them, throwing long shadows across the press. His eyes darted to the wrench on the workbench. His hand twitched.

Paige tilted her head, a silent dare.

The boy's chest rose and fell. He swallowed hard, then snatched the wrench, holding it like a club.
Paige stepped forward, calm as a butcher.

The press creaked again, its gears shifting with the faintest metallic whine. The boy's grip tightened.
And then he charged. The boy came at her with the wrench raised high. His shadow leapt across the rafters,

stretched long and wild by the lanternlight. His boots hammered the floorboards like a drumroll.

Paige waited until he was nearly on her, then stepped aside, fast and precise. She caught his wrist mid-swing and twisted. The wrench clattered to the floor, ringing like a bell. His cry cracked the silence, sharp and desperate. She shoved him forward, his chest slamming against the press. The machine groaned, the nails and chain she had planted grinding into the gears.

For a moment, the room was quiet except for his wheezing breath. Then the press seized him. His sleeve snagged, the fabric pulled tight. He jerked backward, but Paige planted her hand on the back of his neck and held him steady.

The gears began to turn. Slowly at first, then with hunger.

The boy screamed. His arm was dragged into the rollers, skin and bone grinding inch by inch. The iron teeth chewed through fabric, then flesh. Wood creaked, metal shrieked, and the press pulled harder.

Paige stepped back and let him struggle. His eyes locked on hers, wide and wet in the lantern glow. His mouth opened in a plea, but the sound cut off when the rollers snapped his elbow like a twig. Blood splattered across the parchment, marbling Franklin's declarations in red.

The press kept going. It always kept going.

His chest hit the gears. Ribs snapped, lungs collapsed with a wet crunch. His scream strangled into a gurgle. The rollers turned his body into pulp, spitting meat and cloth, until what had been a boy was nothing but ruin pressed flat against Franklin's altar.

The sound was obscene: bones grinding, tendons tearing, the steady rhythm of industry turned butcher. The smell filled the air, hot blood mixing with ink and grease until the room stank of copper and smoke.

Paige crouched, picked up the wrench slick with his sweat, and jammed it into the gears. The machine shrieked. Sparks burst in the lantern glow. The corpse was dragged deeper, skull splitting against the rollers, blood spraying across the hanging sheets. The words *life, liberty, happiness* blurred into black and red slurry.

Paige didn't blink. She just watched. From outside, faint voices still hovered. The younger apprentices hadn't run far.

"…he's dead."
"…we have to tell someone."
"…what if she comes out?"

Their terror vibrated in the alley like strings plucked too tight. Paige strode to the door and kicked it wide. Smoke and blood rolled out into the night.

The boys froze mid-step. Their eyes went wide when they saw her, framed in the doorway with lanternlight and fire at her back, blood dripping from her fingers.

Behind her, the press groaned, still chewing their friend into nothing.

They saw the shape on the rollers, the torn fabric, the twitch of one last ruined limb. Their faces went slack with horror.

Paige tilted her head. Her voice was flat, calm, absolute: "Run."

They bolted. Their screams tore through the lane, bouncing off brick walls, calling her a witch, a monster, a devil. The city was already hearing her name before dawn.

Paige turned back inside. The press was locked now, the chain jammed tight, the corpse slumped half-in, half-out. The lantern flickered low. She tipped it, spilling oil. Fire rushed along the floorboards and leapt to the bundles of paper stacked in the corner. Pages curled instantly, words blackening into smoke.

The flames raced upward, devouring broadsides strung across the rafters. *Freedom, equality, independence* curled into ash. Franklin's sermons vanished in seconds. The room roared, hot and alive.

Paige stood in the center, letting the fire paint her in orange and red. She didn't flinch when the corpse caught, the fat sizzling, the hair burning. She watched it until the press itself groaned and buckled, the machine choking on its own sacrifice.

Satisfied, she tucked the bloody wrench into her belt beside Jefferson's quill. Another tool stolen, another altar broken.

She walked out into the street just as the first window burst, glass exploding across the cobblestones. Neighbors shouted and ran with buckets. The alarm bell clanged. Smoke coiled into the night sky.

The crowd saw her emerge. Black streaks of soot marked her face, her hands still wet with blood. She walked slow, unhurried, through the chaos. A woman pulled her child back. A man raised his hand, pointing, whispering, "Witch." None came closer.

Ash drifted down like black snow. One page landed at her feet. She picked it up, Franklin's face half-burned, his printed smile warped into a sneer. She crushed it in her fist and let the ashes slip through her fingers.

Paige adjusted her belt and kept walking. Her boots struck the stones with steady rhythm. Behind her, the shop roared like a dying beast, Franklin's words reduced to smoke.

She turned into an alley and disappeared into shadow.

The crowd parted in her wake. No one dared follow. They whispered instead, fear thick in their voices, her name carried on the wind.

And at the far end of the street, another sound cut through the bells and shouts, the slam of a carriage door.

A heavy figure stepped into the firelight, leaning on a cane. His wig was crooked, his face slick with sweat. Benjamin Franklin. He stared at the inferno, his jaw clenched, eyes glittering with fury.

"She thinks she can silence me with fire," he muttered, voice low but sharp enough for those nearest to hear. His hands trembled as he gripped the cane. "No torch will best lightning."

The neighbors turned to look at him, their buckets forgotten, their faces pale. Franklin's gaze never left the flames.

The crowd shivered. Some glanced toward the alley where Paige had vanished. Others stared at Franklin, caught between fear and awe.

"She thinks she can silence me with fire," he muttered. His voice was low, but those nearest leaned in, desperate to hear. "But fire is crude. Fire is chaos." He raised his cane and pointed at the burning press. "I will answer her with order. With proof. With lightning itself."
The onlookers stared. Some shifted uneasily, as though his fury was as dangerous as the blaze.

Franklin's voice hardened. "If she is a witch, science will unmask her. And when it does…" His teeth showed in a grim smile. "…she will burn."

The crowd shivered. Buckets sloshed uselessly in their hands. The bell tolled on, but no one moved.

The fire roared higher, a red wound against the night sky. And Franklin's vow carried louder than the flames.

~4
The Tavern Women

The tavern sat low on the corner, shutters half-broken, its door sagging on tired hinges. The sign above it had been painted years ago, some noble crest long since flaked away, but the locals knew it by smell: sour ale, smoke, sweat, and the tang of grease cooked too long. It was the kind of place where no congressman would ever set foot, which meant it was exactly where Paige belonged.

She slipped inside at dusk. The room was dim, lit by a few guttering candles that burned with more wax than flame. Smoke clung to the rafters. A fire hissed in the hearth, logs soaked through with sap. The patrons were mostly women, not the kind Franklin toasted in his essays about virtue, but the other kind. Widows in threadbare shawls. Prostitutes with bruises yellowing on their arms. Servants who had slipped away from kitchens for a few stolen hours. They sat in clusters, voices low but sharp, their laughter jagged, carrying the weight of exhaustion.

Paige ordered nothing. She slid into a bench near the corner, the shadows wrapping around her. She watched. That was her strength, watching.

A woman with hair pulled tight into a knot leaned across a table. "Liberty?" she spat. "Liberty is a word carved on their teeth while they chew us up."

Another woman, younger, her blouse stained with sweat, snorted. "I served Jefferson myself once. Called me 'child.' I was twenty-two with two kids at home." She slammed her tankard down hard enough to slosh ale onto the table. "If men are born equal, why are mine starving?"

The others laughed bitterly, a sound more like a cough than joy.

Paige let their words settle in her. It wasn't just the Fathers she hunted. It was what they'd built, a cage dressed up as a republic, chains written into law. These women saw it for what it was. She just needed to know whether they would fight it… or sell her out the second the soldiers came knocking.

A door banged in the back, and a tall woman with rolled-up sleeves emerged, balancing two jugs of ale. She carried herself like she'd run the place long before the war talk ever began. Her voice cut through the room: "Drink up. Tomorrow you'll be washing these bastards' boots again."

The women raised their tankards and muttered curses in reply.

Paige studied them. They were rough, worn, but their eyes burned. She could see the spark there, the coals of fury banked under years of silence. She knew sparks well enough to recognize when they might catch.

She leaned forward, speaking for the first time. "You toast them, but do you ever toast yourselves?"

The table nearest her turned. A woman with hollow cheeks squinted. "And who the hell are you?"

Paige shrugged. "No one that matters. Just someone tired of assholes writing the rules."

The room went still. Tankards hovered mid-air. A hush spread. It was dangerous to say what everyone thought. Dangerous, and intoxicating.

The tall woman with the jugs set them down slowly, eyes narrowing. "Talk like that will get you strung up. Or worse."

Paige met her stare. "Worse has already happened." She let the silence stretch, let the words sink in. Then she leaned back against the wall. "I've seen men fall. They're not as untouchable as they'd have you think."

The room crackled with unease. The women looked at one another, measuring her. Some suspicious, some curious, all of them hungry for something they couldn't yet name.

From outside came the jangle of spurs. Laughter, men's laughter, drunk and mean. The tavern stiffened like a body bracing for a blow.

The door slammed open.

Three soldiers swaggered in, uniforms loose, muskets slung careless over their shoulders. Their boots clattered on the floorboards, their faces already flushed with drink. The stench of sweat and rum wafted in with them.

The tallest one grinned, revealing a row of crooked teeth. "Evening, ladies. Thought we'd come warm our hands by your fire."

They spread out, moving between the tables like wolves sniffing meat. One soldier grabbed a tankard from a woman's hand and downed it in a gulp. Another leaned too close to a girl barely more than fifteen, his fingers brushing her hair. She flinched. The room went rigid.

Paige sat very still, watching. This was the test. Would these women fight, or would they lower their eyes, take the abuse, and hope the soldiers left before things got worse?

The soldier with the crooked teeth leaned over the bar, leering at the tall woman with the jugs. "Pour us a drink, sweetheart. Or we'll take it another way."

The barmaid didn't move. Her hands were steady on the wood. Her eyes flicked, once, toward Paige in the corner.

Paige said nothing. She let the tension stretch, the silence crackle. The women shifted in their seats, fingers brushing knives, tankards, pokers pulled from the fire. Their fury was there, right under the skin, but so was fear.

The crooked-tooth soldier slammed his fist on the counter. "Did you hear me?"

The sound echoed. The fire popped. The room held its breath.

Paige's hand rested on the knife at her belt. Not yet. Not until they moved.

The soldier closest to the girl with the braid bent lower, his breath hot on her ear. "Smile for me." His hand closed around her wrist.

The girl jerked away, eyes wide, tankard clutched in her other hand.

Paige's gaze swept the room. Every woman's eyes were locked on that scene. Every jaw was clenched. The air was thick with something sharp, ready to snap.

The barmaid broke it.

"Pour your own damn drink," she said. Her voice was calm, but steel threaded through it.

The soldiers laughed, a nasty sound. The crooked-tooth man shoved her hard enough to rattle the bottles on the shelf.

That was the moment. The room quivered on the edge of violence. The women looked to Paige, not because they knew her, but because they saw her sitting there, unafraid. A signal in the dark.

Paige met their eyes, one by one, and gave the smallest nod.

The girl with the braid tightened her grip on her tankard. The barmaid's hand drifted to the iron poker by the fire. Another woman slipped a knife from beneath her apron.

The soldiers didn't see it yet. They were laughing, jeering, drunk on their own power. But Paige knew. The spark had caught.

The crooked-tooth soldier still had his hand on the barmaid's shoulder when the room broke.

It started with the youngest one, the girl with the braid. She swung her tankard with both hands, catching the soldier who had been pawing her. The mug slammed into his jaw with a hollow crack. His head snapped sideways, teeth flying, ale and blood spraying across the table. He staggered back, hands clutching his mouth, eyes wild with shock.

The room gasped, then roared.

The second soldier reached for his musket, but the barmaid had already grabbed the iron poker from the hearth. She swung it in a vicious arc, the glowing tip smashing into his temple. The smell of burnt flesh hit the air as he collapsed, twitching, his musket clattering across the floor.

The third soldier spun, grabbing the youngest girl by the arm. He raised his fist, and Paige moved. She was across the room in three strides. Her knife flashed once, slicing his wrist open to the bone. His hand dropped uselessly, blood pouring down his sleeve. He bellowed,

stumbling back, but Paige didn't finish him. She
stepped aside.

The women swarmed.

A widow with sunken cheeks jabbed a broken bottle
into his gut again and again. A prostitute with wild eyes
drove her knife into his thigh, twisting until he fell.
They kicked and clawed, voices rising not in fear but in
fury, years of silence erupting all at once.

The first soldier tried to crawl toward the door, his jaw
dangling, teeth scattered like dice across the
floorboards. The girl with the braid planted her boot on
his back, lifted her tankard high, and brought it down
on his skull. Once. Twice. The sound was wet, final.

The one with the scorched face tried to get up, but the
barmaid smashed the poker down again, harder, until
his head cracked against the floor. The fire hissed with
the spray of his blood.

The third soldier, already gutted, gurgled and thrashed
until the widow's blade stilled him. His blood spread
across the planks, soaking the women's skirts, pooling
around their boots.

And then, silence.

The fire crackled. The women panted, faces flushed,
hands dripping red. The soldiers lay broken on the
tavern floor, one without a jaw, one with his head
scorched open, one carved apart like meat on a
butcher's block.

Paige stood in the middle of it, knife slick, watching them. She hadn't needed to give the order. They had done it themselves.

The barmaid was the first to speak. Her voice shook, but it carried. "Well. That was overdue."

The women laughed, raw and jagged, the sound of a wound torn open. They weren't delicate. They weren't horrified. They were alive in the aftermath, breathless with the shock of finally striking back.

The girl with the braid looked down at her bloodied tankard, then at Paige. "What now?"

Paige wiped her blade on the dead soldier's coat. "Now you drink."

The line cut the tension. The barmaid barked a laugh, grabbed an unbroken jug, and poured. She sloshed ale into mugs, ignoring the blood smeared across the wood. The women raised their drinks with shaking hands.

"To us," one said.

"To no more masters," another added.

They clinked their tankards over the corpses, ale spilling into the blood. They drank deep, some choking on laughter, some on tears.

Paige lifted her mug last. She didn't smile. She didn't join the laughter. She raised it once, a grim salute, and drank.

The fire in the hearth hissed, the only witness to the toast.

But even as the women cheered, Paige's eyes were elsewhere. She scanned the room, the windows, the street beyond. Already she could hear faint sounds outside, a cart passing, footsteps slowing, whispers carrying through the cracks in the shutters. Word of soldiers killed here would spread before dawn. And once it spread, the city would want someone to blame.

The barmaid must have felt it too. She leaned on the counter, her tankard clutched tight, and said quietly, "They'll come for us."

The widow nodded. "They'll call it murder. They'll call it rebellion."

"They'll call it witchcraft," muttered the girl with the braid. Her voice was hollow, but her grip on the tankard didn't loosen.

All eyes turned to Paige.

Paige didn't answer. She set her mug down on the table, the sound sharp in the silence. It cut through the laughter like a blade. She looked at each of them in turn, at their bloodied hands gripping mugs too tightly, at their flushed faces slick with sweat, at the eyes that still burned hot from the killing. She saw the question etched across every face though none dared voice it: *are we safe with you, or damned?*

Finally, she spoke. "Now they know it isn't just me."

The words landed heavy as stone. Not a comfort. Not a promise. Just a fact.

The women shifted uneasily. Some nodded slow, fire still alive in their gaze, ready to carry it further. Others paled, reality settling in like ash falling after a blaze, the weight of what they had done, what it would cost them. The silence thickened, pressing against their throats. Between them hung a choice: to stand with her and burn, or to turn her in and beg mercy from men who had never given it.

Paige stepped back into the shadows, knife still slick, her expression unreadable.

The women raised their mugs again, but this time without words. They drank in silence, the only sound the drip of blood on the floorboards, pooling around the corpses cooling at their feet.

~5
Jefferson's Last Supper

Monticello rose from the Virginia hills like a smug grin cut into the earth. The dome gleamed in the moonlight, white columns framed in shadow, lanterns flickering across polished windows. It was a mansion dressed as a republic, the home of a man who wrote about liberty while children fetched his slippers.

Paige moved silent through the trees that bordered the estate. The night air was thick with the smell of summer grass and the faint stink of the smokehouses. Somewhere in the distance a whip cracked, followed by muffled sobs. Dogs barked once, then fell quiet.

She crouched low at the edge of the lawn. The house pulsed with light, not quiet sleep but celebration. Laughter drifted through the night, brittle and arrogant. A feast was underway. Jefferson was dining.

Paige studied the guards first. Two at the front steps, muskets slung, half-drunk already from the sound of their slurred voices. Another paced along the veranda, boots scuffing against marble. Lanterns swung from iron hooks, spilling light across the manicured path. Out back, shadows moved near the kitchen door, more guards, waiting, restless.

It was a fortress built not with stone but with bodies, enslaved children running trays of food, women carrying buckets, men hauling casks of wine. All of them moving silently, efficiently, their eyes cast down.

Inside, Jefferson's voice carried, smooth and smug. "The world is watching, gentlemen. And the world will learn from us." His laughter followed, high and self-satisfied.

Paige adjusted the knife at her belt and slipped across the grass. She hugged the shadows of the hedges, skirt brushing dew-soaked leaves, boots barely making a sound. When one guard turned his head to spit into the dirt, she was already past him, a phantom sliding against the wall.

At the kitchen entrance she paused. The door stood ajar, heat and noise pouring out, the clatter of pans, the hiss of roasting meat, the whispers of women too exhausted to speak full sentences. She slipped inside.

The kitchen was chaos: fire roaring in the hearth, sweat streaming down the faces of boys turning spits, women chopping, stirring, hauling. No one looked at her. To them, she was just another shadow in the endless work.

A girl no older than twelve carried a tray of glasses past her. Paige caught her eye for a second. The girl froze, gaze flicking to the knife at Paige's belt, then back up. Paige gave the faintest nod. The girl's lip trembled, but she didn't scream. She just walked on, faster now, tray rattling in her hands.

Paige followed her path into the hall. The dining room spread out in candlelit splendor. A long polished table gleamed with silverware, crystal glasses, platters heavy with roasted meats, bowls of fruit, decanters of wine. Enslaved children hovered behind chairs, pouring, fetching, bowing low at every command. And at the head sat Jefferson.

Thomas Jefferson reclined in his chair like a king pretending not to be one. His wig sat perfectly powdered, his coat embroidered in gold. His thin smile spread as he spoke, hand gesturing lazily with a goblet of wine. "Liberty is not the property of the mob, gentlemen. It must be stewarded. Guided. Written, as we have written it, with order and reason."

The men around him nodded, muttering agreement, their mouths stuffed with meat. Laughter punctured the air like knives. Paige lingered at the edge of the shadows, watching.

Jefferson leaned back, letting a boy no older than ten refill his glass. He ran his hand over the child's head absently, like one might stroke a dog. The boy didn't flinch, but Paige saw the tightness in his jaw, the way his fingers gripped the bottle too hard.

Jefferson raised his glass. "To the republic. To the order we have built. To the prosperity we will enjoy."

The men cheered. Glasses clinked. Wine spilled down their chins. Paige's hand rested on her knife. Not yet.

The guards lined the walls now. Four of them, muskets gleaming in the candlelight. Their eyes swept the room, bored but alert. One yawned. Another scratched at his beard. But they were there, and they were armed. Jefferson's eyes flicked toward the shadows. For a second, Paige thought he saw her. His smile tightened, and he leaned closer to the man beside him.

"She'll come," Jefferson murmured, just loud enough for Paige to hear. His lips barely moved. "She cannot resist a stage such as this."

The man frowned. "Who?"

"The witch," Jefferson whispered. "The phantom they whisper of in Philadelphia. She desecrates words, presses, even Congress itself. Do you think she will leave me untouched?" His smile widened, smug, certain. "No. She will come. And when she does, we will be ready."

The man shifted uncomfortably, glancing toward the guards. Paige's blood cooled. He suspected. He wanted her here. This was a trap. But traps cut both ways.

She slipped further into the room, staying in the shadows of the drapes. The smell of roasted pig filled her nose, rich and greasy. The head still sat on the platter, apple in its mouth, glazed skin shining under the candlelight.

Jefferson carved a slice, holding it up with a smile. "Gentlemen, tonight we feast not just on meat, but on destiny itself. We are shaping the future. We are the architects of eternity."

The table roared with drunken approval. Paige's fingers tightened around the knife. Not yet. Her eyes flicked to the enslaved children moving silently around the table. Their faces were blank masks, but their eyes burned when they looked at Jefferson, when they looked at the guards. They were the silent witnesses. They were her cover.

Jefferson lifted his fork, raised it in a mock salute, and took a bite of the pig's flesh. Grease dripped down his chin. He dabbed it with a napkin, never breaking his smile.

"Yes," he murmured. "She will come. And when she does, she will see what liberty looks like in the hands of reason."

The guards shifted. One adjusted his musket strap. Another glanced toward the door. The room tensed, just for a second, as though even they felt the weight of his words. Paige waited. Her heart beat steady, slow. She had learned patience long ago. Let him gloat. Let him savor. The fall would be sharper when it came.

A boy dropped a glass. It shattered against the floor. The sound cracked the air. Everyone froze. Jefferson's head snapped toward the child, fury twisting his features.

"You clumsy little savage," he hissed, raising his hand.

Paige moved closer. Still hidden, still waiting. Jefferson's hand hung in the air. The boy cowered, eyes wide. The moment stretched like wire pulled taut. Paige's knife glinted in the candlelight. The trap was set. But not for her.

The boy froze under Jefferson's raised hand. The broken glass still glittered on the floor, and the silence stretched taut.

"Ungrateful little beast," Jefferson hissed. His fingers curled into a fist, his powdered wig bobbing as he leaned down.

"Touch him," Paige said, stepping out of the shadows, "and I'll cut your hand off at the wrist."

The words sliced the room in half.

Gasps. Forks dropped. Men surged from their chairs, tripping over themselves. The enslaved children froze where they stood, pitchers of wine trembling in their hands. The guards jolted upright, muskets snapping to attention.

And at the head of the table, Jefferson leaned back slowly into his chair. His lips curled into a smile.

"Ah," he said, voice smooth, "I wondered how long you'd let me wait."

His eyes gleamed with smug triumph, as if he'd conjured her himself.

The boy stared at Paige, wide-eyed, breath trapped in his throat. The other children watched, terrified, caught between hope and horror.

"Seize her!" one guard barked. Muskets rose, bayonets catching the candlelight.

Paige didn't flinch. She stood at the edge of the feast, knife loose at her side, eyes locked on Jefferson.

Jefferson raised his hand lazily. "Not yet." His voice carried calm command, smug authority. The guards froze at once.

"She'll speak," Jefferson said, gaze still fixed on Paige. "She'll justify herself before history."

Paige tilted her head. "You mean before your dinner guests?"

Laughter rippled, brittle and forced, from the men at the table.

Jefferson spread his hands, still smiling. "Without men like me, there is no republic. No liberty. No order. I've written the words that will outlive us all. And you," he leaned forward, eyes narrowing, "you're just chaos with a blade."

Paige's smile was cold. "Chaos is honest. Your words are chains dipped in ink."

The guards shifted uneasily. The men at the table muttered among themselves. Some nodded at Jefferson's pomp. Others glanced at Paige with something darker in their eyes.

Jefferson's voice rose, loud enough to drown them. "She burns presses, slaughters boys, stabs at parchment. She wants to drag us back into savagery. You see her knife, but do you see the truth? She is no liberty. She is death itself."

The words hung in the air like smoke.

Paige's voice cut through it: "And what do you call this?" She gestured toward the children lining the walls, the girls hauling trays, the boys pouring wine. "Order? Prosperity? Freedom?"

Her tone was sharp, scathing. "You polish your rot and call it reason. But it's still rot."

For the first time, Jefferson's smile twitched.

"Kill her," he spat. The guards moved.

Bayonets glinted. Paige hurled her knife. It sank into the roasted pig's skull with a crack. Grease spilled across the polished wood. The crash startled them, enough for her to move.

She lunged. Her fist smashed a guard's throat. He gagged as she tore the musket from his grip and swung it like a club, shattering another man's jaw.

Chairs toppled. Glass burst. The children huddled in corners, covering their ears.

A bayonet jabbed. Paige seized the arm, snapped it until bone cracked, then drove her knee into his face.

A pistol fired wide, shattering a wine bottle. She slammed the shooter's head into the table, dragging his face across platters until blood streaked the bread and fruit. His scream was drowned by the roar of flames as a curtain caught, smoke thickening.

Another staggered up. Paige smashed the musket stock into his temple. He collapsed.

Silence. Guards sprawled broken across the carpet. Food mingled with blood, wine dripping like veins across the cloth.

Jefferson stood alone, pale but furious, hand hovering near the carving knife in the pig. His voice cracked but rose in desperation: "You think you can unmake me? I am the author of liberty! Without me there is no nation!"

Paige stepped closer, boots crunching glass. "Without you," she said, "there's finally a chance."

He lunged. Paige caught his wrist, slammed his head into the pig, grease smearing across his face. His muffled curses choked off as she drove his own quill into his throat. Blood spurted, bubbling with his breath, red mingling with the slick fat of the feast.

"Write your last declaration," she whispered. He convulsed once, twice, then sagged lifeless, cheek buried in the roasted flesh.

Paige carved into the table with his knife, each gouge deliberate, slow:

THE MISSING PROSPERITY

No one stopped her. The guests pressed against the walls, pale, trembling. Some whispered prayers, others curses. One man vomited into a wine jug. Another fainted where he stood. The children stared, wide-eyed, as if seeing both salvation and damnation in one figure.

By the time she reached the veranda, the estate was stirring. Dogs barked wild in the distance. Servants muttered behind half-open doors, crossing themselves, terrified she might glance their way. Guards shouted in confusion but none dared enter.

Inside, Jefferson slumped over his feast, blood pooling with grease, the carved words gleaming like a curse. The stench of meat, wine, and death clung to the air. The guests whispered of vengeance, but their voices cracked with fear. They already knew the truth.

Paige walked into the night, unhurried, the quill slick with blood. One Father down.

~6
Addams Gets Dragged

Boston smelled of salt and smoke, the harbor wind carrying brine through the crooked streets. Cobblestones were slick with mud and horse piss, alleys crowded with barrels and fish guts. Yet the square at the center was packed shoulder to shoulder, citizens pressed together like kindling waiting for a spark.

John Adams stood on the steps of the courthouse, his frame rigid, his eyes fever-bright. He raised his arms like a preacher above a congregation, his voice carrying over the restless murmur of the crowd.

"She is a blight upon us!" he thundered. "A creature of chaos who defiles our words, our institutions, our very liberty!"

His voice cracked, but the crowd roared. Farmers in rough coats, apprentices with soot-streaked faces, wives clutching their children closer. They had gathered not for trade or gossip but for spectacle.

"She walks among us with a blade," Adams went on, his lips curling. "She desecrates the work of honest men. She mocks the Lord's providence. And you, "He jabbed a finger at the crowd, "you have seen the fires she leaves in her wake. Will you let her damn us all?"

The mob bellowed as one, fists in the air, voices echoing between stone walls. Someone hurled a stone skyward.

It clattered harmlessly on the steps, but the act sent ripples through the mass, energy like static snapping from body to body.

Adams thrived on it. He paced the steps, red-faced, jowls quivering with passion. "She has slain Jefferson, torn apart the Congress with her witchcraft, brought Franklin low. She is not liberty, she is pestilence! And we will not suffer her!"

Cries rose in answer. "Witch!" "Devil!" "Hang her!"

Children climbed barrels to see. Women shouted hoarse. Men gripped cudgels and ropes. The frenzy thickened like storm clouds gathering. And in the press of bodies, Paige watched.

She leaned against a shadowed wall at the edge of the square, hood drawn low. Her eyes swept the crowd: the trembling hands clutching rope, the sweat-slick brows of men eager to be unleashed, the women caught between fear and fury. The air vibrated with bloodlust.

Adams thrust his fist skyward. "If she shows her face here, we shall deliver her to judgment! We shall chain her, drag her through these streets, and watch her burn!"

The mob cheered, voices shaking windowpanes. Paige's lips curved in a thin smile. She stepped forward, slow, deliberate, boots striking cobblestones with an audible rhythm. The crowd parted instinctively, though no one recognized her yet. They only felt the shift, the way noise faltered, breath caught, the way shadows seemed to follow her.

Adams saw it. His eyes locked on her figure as she emerged into the square. His face drained pale for a heartbeat before rage painted it crimson again.

"There!" he shrieked, voice cracking. "There she stands! The witch herself! Do not falter, seize her!"

The mob turned, hundreds of eyes fixing on Paige. Whispers raced through them, a hiss of rumor and recognition. Paige said nothing. She kept walking, steady, calm, until she stood at the base of the courthouse steps, looking up at Adams. The crowd held its breath.

Adams puffed his chest, pointing down at her. "Do you deny it? Do you deny the blood on your hands, the chaos you've sown? The devil's daughter walks among us!"

Paige tilted her head, meeting his glare. Her voice was low, even, but it carried. "You think they follow you because they believe in you. They don't. They follow because they're afraid."

Murmurs rippled. Men shifted uneasily.
Adams slammed his fist on the rail. "Do not listen to her lies! She would poison your ears as she has poisoned our land!"

Paige's eyes swept the mob, then back to Adams. "No lies. You see it. Every man you've raised on a pedestal has fallen. One by one. And now you stand alone, screaming on your steps, terrified they'll see you for what you are."

Gasps. A woman covered her mouth. An apprentice spat in the dirt but didn't move closer.

Adams shook with fury. "Bind her! Chain her! Drag her!"

But the mob hesitated. They looked from Adams to Paige, their frenzy faltering.

Paige let the silence stretch, tension winding tighter, her hand resting lightly on the hilt of her knife but not drawing it. "Go on," she said softly. "See if they obey you. See if they choose you, or me."

The words landed like stones dropped into water. The crowd shifted, restless, torn.

Adams bellowed louder, desperation seeping through. "She will damn your wives! She will butcher your sons! She will tear your very souls!"

Paige raised her chin, eyes cold. "I don't need to damn them. You've done that yourself."

The crowd erupted, shouts, arguments, fists shaking not just at Paige but at Adams, too. The frenzy was turning, the energy unstable. It teetered on a knife's edge.

Adams saw it slipping. His voice broke into a scream. "Seize her! Now!"

But no one moved.

Paige took another step forward. "You talk of liberty, Adams. But I wonder, when they look back, will they remember your speeches, or will they remember your fear?"

His face twisted. Spittle flew. He reached for a musket propped by the door, hands trembling. The mob gasped. Paige didn't move, her eyes locked on his, waiting.

The tension was unbearable. The square seemed to shrink, time slowing, every heart hammering in unison. The mob balanced between riot and mutiny, their eyes darting between Adams' rage and Paige's calm. Paige's lips curved again, the faintest smile. She whispered, just loud enough for him to hear: "Without you, they'll finally have a chance."

Adams roared, musket clutched to his chest. But when he turned to the crowd for support, he saw doubt staring back at him, hesitation, uncertainty, fear. The seed had been planted. The frenzy would turn. And Paige knew it.

She stepped back just enough, letting the fire smolder, letting the tension climb higher. She didn't need to strike yet. Adams was unraveling himself, and soon, the mob would decide who they truly wanted to drag through the streets.

Adams gripped the musket so tightly his knuckles whitened. His eyes darted over the sea of faces in front of him, searching for the blind devotion he had commanded only moments ago. Instead, he saw doubt. Restless murmurs, shifting feet, hands loosening on their ropes and cudgels.

"No!" he barked, desperation cracking his voice. "Don't falter now! Bind her! Drag her through these streets! Do it, or you're cowards unworthy of liberty!"

The mob stirred, but it was not the fervent roar he wanted. It was unease, suspicion, the edge of mutiny.

Paige didn't move. She stood at the base of the courthouse steps, still as stone, eyes fixed on him like a hunter watching an animal that had already limped into the snare.

"Do it!" Adams screamed again. "For your wives, your children, your nation! For me!"
A stone flew, not at Paige, but at him. It struck the wall beside his head, sending plaster dust over his shoulder. Adams froze. His lips trembled.

The crowd rippled with gasps, then laughter, nervous, brittle, but laughter all the same. Paige tilted her head, lips curling in the faintest smile.

"Looks like they made a choice," she said.

Adams' face twisted, red as boiled meat. He raised the musket, aiming at her chest.

But a hand from the crowd shot out, yanking the weapon down. Another grabbed his sleeve. Then another.

Adams sputtered, "Unhand me! Traitors! You'll burn for this!"

But the mob surged. Rough hands dragged him down the courthouse steps, his wig askew, his coat tearing at the seams. His musket clattered across the stones. The square erupted in chaos, not a unified chant, not the frenzy he had stoked, but something darker, more primal.

They dragged him by his arms, by his legs, by his cloak. His shouts turned to shrieks. "I am John Adams! A Father of Liberty! You cannot..."

A fist smashed into his mouth, cutting the words short. Blood sprayed across his chin. His front teeth clattered onto the cobblestones, gleaming white against the mud. The crowd howled, half laughter, half rage.

They threw a rope around his ankles and pulled. Adams hit the ground face-first, his cry muffled by dirt. They began to drag him down the street, his head bouncing off the cobblestones with each lurch. Skin split. Blood smeared. His wig came loose, trampled underfoot.

Paige followed at a distance, hands loose at her sides, silent. She didn't need to direct this. The mob had taken her spark and turned it into a fire.

Adams screamed again, voice shredding. "Stop! Stop this madness! I am law! I am order!"

A boot came down on his back. A boy no older than twelve swung a cudgel into his ribs. The crack of bone echoed. Adams wheezed, spitting blood. The rope jerked him forward again. His face scraped along the stones, leaving a crimson trail. Women spat on him as he passed, some slapping his face with open hands, others hurling scraps of rotten food.

"Witch," someone hissed, not at Paige this time, but at him. The word stuck, turned back against its master.

Adams clawed at the rope, but every time he tried to free himself, someone yanked harder. His nails tore bloody against the fibers. Paige's boots crunched steadily behind the mob. She watched, her face unreadable. This wasn't mercy, wasn't vengeance, it was inevitability.

The rope dragged him past the tavern, where women leaned out the windows, jeering. One dumped a pot of boiling water. Adams screamed as it splashed across his back, blistering his skin. The mob cheered.

They pulled him down to the docks, the stench of fish and salt heavy in the air. Adams gasped, face swollen, lips torn. His fine clothes were rags now, smeared with blood and filth. He tried to speak again, voice rasping, broken: "Please…"

No one listened.

The rope tightened. With a violent tug, they hauled him across the planks, head cracking against the wood. He gurgled, choking on blood.

Someone shouted, "To the harbor!"

The mob roared. They dragged him to the edge of the pier, his body limp, face pulped and unrecognizable. For a moment, he dangled there, held up only by the rope around his ankles, swaying over the black water.

"Law," he whispered hoarsely, barely audible. "Order."

The rope jerked. They plunged him into the harbor. The crowd erupted in cheers as the water swallowed him. He thrashed weakly, bubbles foaming at the surface, before his head disappeared beneath the waves. The rope tugged, pulling him under again and again, each dunk slower than the last.

When at last they pulled him up, Adams' body flopped onto the dock like a gutted fish, chest rising in shallow, pitiful gasps. Paige stepped closer now, through the parting mob. She crouched by his ruined face. His one good eye fluttered open, blood dripping down his cheek.

She leaned in, her voice low, cold. "This is the liberty you built, dragged through mud, drowned in filth. They don't need me to kill you. You did it yourself."

His lips moved, but no sound came.

Paige stood, turned, and left him there, sprawled and broken before the jeering mob. They weren't done.

A chain appeared, hauled from a shipyard. Someone looped it around his legs. With a roar, they dragged him again, this time through the market, his body bouncing lifelessly. Bones snapped audibly. Blood smeared across stalls. Children screamed and laughed all at once.

Paige didn't follow now. She turned into an alley, letting the sound of their frenzy trail behind her like smoke. Her boots struck cobblestones in steady rhythm, unhurried.

By the time she reached the edge of the square again, Adams' body was gone, swallowed by the mob. Only the echo of their roars remained. Whispers replaced them.

"She made them turn."
"They saw him for what he was."
"She doesn't even need the blade. Just the truth."

Paige adjusted the quill at her belt, slick with dried blood. She walked on, disappearing into the labyrinth of Boston's crooked streets, leaving the city to reckon with what it had done. One more Father down.

~7
Lightening Franklin

The sky over Philadelphia turned the color of lead. Clouds hung heavy and dark, their edges bruised violet where the last sunlight struggled through. The air smelled of rain and iron, charged with something more than weather.

A crowd filled the square outside Franklin's house, men in coats, women clutching shawls, children balanced on barrels to see. The rumor had spread like fire: Franklin, the great mind, the sage, was about to prove once and for all that the woman who haunted the city was no patriot, no rebel, but a witch.

At the center of it all, Franklin stood on a raised platform. His hair was wild, his spectacles gleaming in the dim light, his voice carrying over the restless murmurs. He held a key strung to a length of wire, the other end disappearing into the storm clouds above where a kite flapped and snapped in the wind.

"Citizens!" he boomed. "You have heard the tales. You have seen the wreckage left in her wake. She tears at our institutions, strikes down our leaders, mocks liberty itself. Tonight, we shall test her nature before God and science alike!"

The crowd roared, some jeering, some praying under their breath.

Paige watched from the shadows at the edge of the square, hood low, eyes fixed on him. This was no tavern brawl, no backroom ambush. Franklin had chosen the stage, the audience, the weapon. He had chosen the storm itself.

Her jaw tightened. The trap was elegant in its arrogance.

Franklin raised the key high, the metal glinting. "If she is flesh and blood, she will fall as any mortal would. But if she is what she appears, a devil's handmaid, the lightning will reveal her!"

Murmurs rippled. Women clutched children closer. Men spat in the dirt, eager for spectacle.

Guards ringed the platform, muskets ready. They weren't there to protect Franklin, they were there to ensure Paige could not slip away once she revealed herself.

The wind gusted, carrying a low rumble of thunder. The kite jerked violently against its string.

Paige stepped forward into the open.

A ripple ran through the crowd, gasps, curses, shouts. People parted instinctively, shrinking back even as curiosity locked their eyes on her.

Franklin's face split into a grin. "Ah. She comes. Just as I said she would."

Paige walked slowly, deliberately, until she stood at the foot of the platform. Her eyes never left him.

"You think lightning will save you?" she said, voice low but clear.

Franklin's laugh was sharp, edged with madness. "Not save, my dear. Prove. You see, words are flimsy things. They burn, they twist. But the heavens, they do not lie. They strike where truth demands."

He gestured to the storm. Thunder rolled, closer now.

Paige tilted her head. "And you think you can command the sky."

"I already have!" he thundered. "I pulled fire from it once. I will do so again, and tonight the people will see you for what you are!"

The crowd murmured approval, some shouting, "Witch! Witch!" Others looked uneasy, eyes darting between the storm and the calm figure of the woman who had walked unafraid into it.

Paige glanced at the wire, at the key swaying in Franklin's grip. She could smell the charge, taste it on her tongue like copper. It would not take much, a spark, a strike, and she would be ash on the cobblestones.

The guards shifted, tense, waiting.

Franklin's grin widened. "Kneel, witch, and let the heavens pass judgment."

Paige did not kneel. She folded her arms, eyes on him, unblinking. "You call this judgment. I call it desperation."

His smile faltered for a fraction, then hardened. "Desperation? No. This is science. This is progress. This is the end of your terror."

The crowd shouted again, emboldened. "End her! Burn her!"

Franklin thrust the key higher, shaking it at the clouds. "Now!" he bellowed. "Now, Lord! Now, nature! Strike her down!"

The sky rumbled in answer, a jagged line of lightning flashing across the horizon. A collective gasp rippled through the square.

Paige's muscles coiled, ready. She could feel the charge thickening, the hairs on her arms rising. The storm was close.

Franklin's eyes gleamed with triumph. "There it is! The very heavens cry out against her!"

Paige's gaze flicked to the wire again. The arrogance of it. He thought he could wield the storm as easily as ink on paper. He thought nature would obey his command, just as he expected the people to.

But storms had no masters.

The first drop of rain struck the back of her hand, hot against her skin. Then another. Then a sheet of it, driving hard, soaking the square in seconds.

The crowd shrieked and ducked for cover, but none fled. They wanted to see. They wanted blood or fire or both.

Franklin's voice rose over the downpour. "Behold! Let lightning reveal her! Let the witch burn!"

Thunder cracked, so loud it rattled the teeth of everyone in the square. The kite above snapped and twisted, wire quivering in Franklin's grip. The key jerked violently, sparking faint blue.

Paige stood unmoving, eyes locked on him, the storm dancing in her pupils.

The suspense stretched, unbearable. Every eye flicked between the woman standing silent and the man with a wire to the sky, waiting for fire to fall.

For the first time since arriving in this world, Paige felt the edge of danger that might actually consume her. Not a musket, not a knife, not even a mob, this was the raw force of the earth itself, drawn down by the hand of a man who thought himself untouchable.

Franklin was shouting, half to the sky, half to himself. "Strike! Strike her down! Show them! Prove me right!"

The wire hissed, glowing faintly in the stormlight. Sparks danced at the key.

Paige flexed her fingers at her side. If the lightning struck, she would not survive it. The suspense tightened around her like a noose.

The crowd screamed and pressed closer to the edges of the square, unable to look away.

And Franklin, mad with triumph, raised the key higher still, daring the storm to obey.

The key in Franklin's fist glowed faint blue, sparks skittering off its edges. His spectacles flashed white with each shimmer. He held the wire taut, face turned skyward, shouting at the storm as if he had been promised obedience.

"Now! Show them, Lord! Strike her down!"

The crowd roared in unison, half in awe, half in fear. Some cried "Witch!" while others muttered prayers into their sleeves. Rain poured harder, slicking cobblestones, running into the gutters in black rivulets.

Paige stood still, the water plastering her hair to her face, her eyes locked on him. Every nerve screamed to move, but she didn't. Not yet. If Franklin wanted the sky, she would let him have it.

The storm answered.

A jagged bolt tore across the clouds, thunder shaking the square. The wire shivered, sparks leaping up its length. Franklin's grin widened as the key flared with electric fire.

"There! You see?" he shouted. "Even the heavens rise against her!"

The crowd gasped, shrinking back from the arcs of blue light crawling over his hands. The guards shifted uneasily, muskets trembling in their grip. Paige took one slow step forward.

Franklin's eyes snapped to her. "Stay where you are! The next strike will burn you to ash!"

Paige's lips curved in a thin smile. "Or maybe it'll burn you."

He laughed, manic and sharp. "Me? No, girl. I have mastered this. I have coaxed the storm before. I..."

The wire sparked violently, jerking in his grip. The key hissed, smoke rising from his palm.

Paige took another step forward. "You think the storm serves you. But storms don't kneel. They devour."

Franklin's face twisted, fury and fear flickering across it. "Lies! Witchcraft!"

Another bolt cracked overhead. The wire flared, and Franklin screamed as the current jolted up his arm. His hair stood on end, his jaw clenched so hard his teeth cracked audibly.

The crowd shrieked. Some bolted for cover, others pressed closer, entranced by the sight of the great Franklin writhing under his own "experiment."

Paige moved now. She darted up the platform steps, boots slipping on the rain-slick wood. The guards shouted, muskets lifting, but the storm chose that moment to strike again.

The bolt slammed into the kite above. The wire flared blinding white. The musket barrels sparked in the soldiers' hands, exploding back into their faces. Screams tore the night as the guards collapsed, bleeding and burned.

Paige reached Franklin. He staggered, smoke rising from his clothes, still clutching the key like a talisman. His skin blistered where the wire bit into it, but he refused to let go.

"You... will not... take me!" he snarled through gritted teeth.

Paige grabbed the wire from his other hand and looped it around his wrist before he could resist. His eyes went wide with panic.

"No, no, you don't understand."

But it was too late. The storm came down in full. A bolt split the sky and hammered into the wire. The platform exploded in light. Franklin convulsed, his body jerking like a puppet on snapped strings. His scream was drowned by the thunder, a raw, animal sound that seemed to tear his throat apart.

Blue fire crawled over his skin, searing it black in streaks. His eyes bulged, then burst, spraying blood down his cheeks. His jaw snapped open and shut in spasms, teeth cracking loose one by one.

The crowd screamed and scrambled back as his body glowed white-hot for an instant, then ruptured. Flesh split. Bone shattered. Steam hissed as rain hit his burning skin. The smell of charred meat rolled over the square.

Paige stepped back, unflinching, as Franklin's body shook and split apart. A final bolt arced through him, blowing his skull open in a spray of sparks and blood. His wig burst into flames before being soaked by the downpour. What remained slumped against the platform railing, half a body, smoking, twitching, the wire still hissing where it clung to his arm. The crowd fell silent, stunned.

Paige stood above the wreckage, soaked and calm. Her knife hung loose at her side, though she hadn't needed it. She raised her voice, steady, cutting through the rain.

"This is your Enlightenment. Your science. Your Fathers. See how they burn."

Gasps rippled. Someone muttered, "She killed Franklin." Another whispered, "No, he killed himself."

Paige turned, stepping off the platform. The crowd parted without a word, pressing back as she passed, eyes wide, breaths shallow. No one raised a hand.

Behind her, the storm groaned one last time. Lightning struck the platform again, shattering it in a blast of splinters and smoke. Franklin's remains scattered across the boards, sizzling in the rain. Paige didn't look back.

She walked through the soaked cobblestones, her boots steady, water running down her face in black streaks of soot and blood.

By the time she reached the end of the square, whispers had replaced the silence.

"Three of them now."
"She's hunting the Fathers."
"She's the devil."
"She's justice."

Paige pulled the quill from her belt, still stained with Jefferson's blood. She lifted it briefly, letting the lightning above catch its glint, then tucked it back. The whispers swelled. Fear. Awe. The storm rolled on, thunder fading into the distance, leaving only smoke, rain, and the stench of Franklin's charred flesh.

Paige vanished into the alleys. Three Fathers down. Only Congress remained, armed to the teeth, and terrified.

~8
The Blood Congress

They met at dusk in the hall that had once been holy to them. Candles guttered along the walls, their flames nervous in the draft that slid under the doors and through the cracked panes. The chamber smelled of wax and wool and the sour tang of men who had been afraid for too long. Three chairs stood empty- Jefferson's, Adams's, Franklin's, like teeth knocked out of a grinning skull.

"Order," Hancock rasped, though no one obeyed the word anymore. Muskets leaned against benches. Swords clinked when a man shifted. Boots scuffed. Paper rustled, the thin, papery sound of fear trying to look like procedure.

"Close the gallery," Madison said, not quite looking at the shadows above. "No spectators."

"They've stayed away ever since," another muttered. "Who'd come now? To watch us die?"

A laugh flickered and died. A clerk fumbled with a quill, hands slick. Powder flasks lay in a neat row on a side table beside a brass tinderbox and a crate of shot. The Sergeant-at-Arms paced before the doors, testing the iron bar that could drop across them, jaw working like he was chewing on a prayer.

"She has killed three of our number," Hancock said, louder, forcing the sentence like a blade through gristle. "She hunts us. But we are not—" His voice snagged on a cough. He coughed again, harder, and drank from a glass. "We are not animals to be taken in alleyways. We are the Congress."

The doors thudded as someone outside tried the latch. Every musket lifted an inch. The Sergeant barked, and the latch fell silent.

"Report," Hancock demanded.

A militia captain stepped forward in muddy boots, hat crushed in one fist. "Two squads around the perimeter. We searched the cellars. The roof. The privies. Scribes are dismissed. Doors barred. Windows watched." He took a breath he didn't quite finish. "Sir… the people gather."

"The people?" Madison asked.

"Women. Apprentices. Sailors. Boys. Not a riot. A… crowd." He swallowed. "They're waiting."

"For what?" Hancock snapped.

The captain's eyes flicked to the empty chairs. "To see who survives."

A murmur slid around the room like a snake. Some men crossed themselves. Some touched the stocks of their muskets as if the wood could answer.

Hancock banged the gavel. "Enough." The wood rang
flat. "We will proceed as planned. Resolutions.
Dispatches to the States. Recommendations for
emergency powers." He cleared his throat and did not
read the next line of the agenda, the one that said in a
finer hand: *contingencies in event of her entry*.

Madison stood. His face looked like parchment that had
been folded too many times. "Gentlemen. We have
been unfortunate. But we are not helpless. She thrives
on spectacle. We must deny her the stage."

"The stage is the city," someone said. "The stage is us."

"Then we change the play," Madison replied, and
everyone tried, for a breath, to believe him.

Up in the gallery, behind the carved balustrade and the
heavy curtain that made a draft where none should be,
Paige listened to men try to convince themselves that
they were still the authors of anything. The wood under
her palms was worn smooth by a hundred anxious
hands. She could feel the building's age, the way it
settled into its foundation like an old soldier bracing for
another volley.

She had come while the bell tower still held daylight,
dressed in a porter's coat with a crate on her shoulder.
The guard at the service door had squinted and waved
her in. The crate had not been empty. There were nails
inside, and links of chain, and a spool of tarred cord
coiled like a sleeping snake. She had left the crate under
the steps where no one looked, and taken the snake with
her.

Below, the Sergeant-at-Arms strode to the doors again, checked the iron brackets, tugged the bar up and down. It thudded satisfyingly into its sockets. He did not look up. He had not looked up all evening. Men rarely look where they fear heaven should be.

Paige stepped sideways along the shadowed ledge, soft-footed, until she reached the gallery stair that joined the hall behind a modest door painted the same color as the wall. It had been added after a carpenter's fall, the paint not quite matched. Her fingers found the hairline crack where the new wood met the old. The latch had been meant to keep spectators out. It would keep something else in.

On the floor below, Madison leaned over a map. "We cannot evacuate. It would be read as surrender. Nor can we open the doors once the mob presses close. We must set our own perimeter." He tapped a quivering finger on the edges of Philadelphia as if the city would obey. "Hold lines here, here. Powder conserved. No stray shots. We fire only when we—"

"—see the whites of her eyes?" a delegate said, too loud, then flushed as men glared.

"—are in mortal danger," Madison finished, brittle.

Hancock set down the gavel. "We are in mortal danger now."

A chair scraped. "We could parley."

"With what?" another demanded. "She does not bargain. She marks. She burns."

"Perhaps she wants something," a thin man offered, desperate for reason. "All things have demands."

"She wants us dead," someone else said. "That is the demand."

Lightning breathed somewhere far away, just enough to set the candle flames trembling. No one mentioned Franklin by name. They could all smell the storm that had touched him still clinging to the city's stones. They could smell what it had cooked.

Paige moved again, hand sliding along the baluster until it found the newel post, warm from the heat pocketed under the rafters. She crouched and drew from her coat the tarred cord, thin as her little finger and as patient as time. She measured with her eyes the distance to the powder flasks, to the tinderbox, to the heap of rags under the clerk's desk where a spilled lantern could look like an accident from a distance and intent when the flames found the floor. She did not rush. The fuse would.

Another knock on the doors, a single, hard rap. The room went rigid. The Sergeant lifted the bar a fraction, then slammed it down again, as if reminding the wood who owned it.

"Mister Hancock," the militia captain said, voice hushed now, "I must ask permission to post men inside the hall itself."

Hancock hesitated. He did not want bayonets between him and the door. He did not want to see what he had ordered. He nodded anyway. "So ordered."

Eight militiamen filed in, wet from the humid dark, muskets bristling. Their boots left small crescents of mud that dried as Paige watched, the way fear dries the mouth. They took positions along the walls, behind the delegates. Two faced the doors. Two watched the windows. Two stood beneath the gallery with their backs to the balustrade and never once lifted their heads.

"Gentlemen," Madison said, louder, steadier, "you must sit. We must act." He held up a list written in a clerk's neat hand. "A resolution condemning the murders. A statement to the people. A call to—"

"—arms?" a voice said from the back, sour with drink and dread.

"To unity," Madison insisted, and the word sounded like something he had once believed in and now could not swallow.

Hancock smoothed the parchment before him. His hands shook. He pinched them still. "Read," he ordered.

The clerk stood. He tried twice before his voice found shape. "Whereas the safety of this Congress is threatened by an assassin… Whereas the commonweal—" He paused, eyes straying to the empty chairs. "Whereas—"

The candles leaned and guttered. A draft slid along the floor, cool, certain. The men shivered and told themselves it was nothing.

Paige eased the thin door of the gallery stair until the latch whispered home. She slid a link of chain through the iron rings that held the bar on the hall side and fed it back around to the stair side, where she could anchor it to the newel. If the Sergeant tried to lift the bar, the chain would keep it honest. She threaded the free end through a loop and pulled until the links sang as they tightened. It was a quiet song, and no one below heard it.

She stood very still and listened to the room live beneath her, the scrape of pens, the coughs swallowed, the tics of men made to sit in their own terror. She let the sound teach her where fear collected and where it overflowed. Fear like this will always try to find an exit. She had just closed one.

A delegate stood abruptly and faced the doors. "We can't sit here and read," he barked. "We must ride out and find her. Or we must run." His face wore the white of a man already running in his mind.

"Sit down," Hancock snapped.

The man didn't. He crossed the aisle toward the Sergeant. "Open these damned doors."

"On whose authority?" the Sergeant asked without turning.

"Mine," the man lied, and reached for the bar.

The Sergeant turned then, slow. He did not lift a hand to stop him. He only stepped aside a fraction, and the man grasped the iron and hauled upward. The bar budged an inch and stopped, chain humming. The man hauled again. The bar answered with a metallic laugh, and the man's breath hissed like a patient's last as the metal refused him.

"What have you done to it?" he demanded, panic already in.

"Nothing," the Sergeant said, and it was not a boast.

Above them, Paige knotted the chain twice and tucked the slack into a shadow you'd need a ladder to inspect. She slid back to the balustrade and peered down.

The hall looked smaller now, crowded with the breath of men who understood, finally, that the building held them the way a jaw holds meat.

"Proceed," Hancock managed, though it sounded like a plea.

The clerk swallowed. "Whereas—"

A child's voice rose outside, high and curious: "Is she in there?"

"Quiet!" someone hissed. "Do you want her to hear?"

"She hears everything," another voice answered, older and certain, and the words came through the crack under the door like a draft.

Paige set a hand to the railing, felt the grain, the gouges left by rings and nails and worry. She thought of Jefferson's table. She thought of Adams's teeth skipping along stone. She thought of Franklin's eyes bursting like blisters under a summer sun. The hall below felt like a lung ready to exhale flame.

She drew the tarred cord from her coat and measured with her eye again: the clerk's desk; the powder flasks; the tinderbox; the fat guttering candle on the edge of Hancock's table, its wax pooling toward the parchment; the heap of rags under the sideboard where a lazy servant had kicked a spill after lunch. She set one end of the cord to the floor behind the gallery stair and fed it through the gap between baluster and post. It slid down like a dark snake onto the wainscoting and then to the floor below, where it kissed the shadow beneath the sideboard and lay very still, as if sleeping.

All it needed was a whisper of fire.

Below, Madison tried to speak over the scrape of chairs and the pulse of breath. "Gentlemen, we only give her what she wants if we panic."

"What does she want?" a voice demanded, raw.

Madison opened his mouth. Closed it. Looked at the empty chairs and, for the first time that night, allowed the truth to cross his face. "An ending," he said.

A musket lifted, not at the doors, but toward the gallery. The militiaman's eyes were red, his jaw clenched so hard the muscle jumped. He stared at the shadows as if he had finally remembered to be afraid of what was above, as well as what was outside.

Paige lay flat behind the balustrade, a dark shape in a darker space. She heard the soldier's breath hiss, felt the attention gather like a hand closing. She waited. The barrel dipped. It dipped because the soldier did not want to be the one who fired the first shot in a room full of powder and men.

She slid a palm along the railing and rose onto her knees, careful as a cat. From her pocket she took a small tin of pitch. Her thumbnail worked the lid. The smell of pine hit her nose, clean and sharp in the stale room. She dabbed the cord. Tar clung, tacky, eager.

Outside, something broke, a bottle, a voice, patience. The crowd pressed closer. Boards groaned. The doors flexed under the bar like a ribcage under a blow.

Hancock flinched. "Sergeant—"

"It holds," the Sergeant said, eyes on the iron. "For now."

Paige anchored the cord near the clerk's desk with a pin tapped into the baseboard. A mouse squeaked and fled. She followed the line with her eyes to where it disappeared under the sideboard and lay against the shadow of rags. She pictured, for a breath, the way flame would crawl when called. It liked edges. It liked drips. It liked old wood more than new.

She put the tin away and drew out flint and steel.

"Don't," Madison said suddenly, not to her, he couldn't see her, but to the men who had begun to shout at one another instead of at the door. "Every shout is tinder."

Paige smiled, a small, private thing.

Hancock scrubbed a hand over his jaw. The gavel looked foolish lying there, a toy among weapons. "If she is here," he said to the room, "show yourself."

Silence argued back.

"She is a coward," someone tried.

"She is a knife," someone answered, too low to name.

Paige leaned the flint against the steel and paused. Not yet. Let the room fill a little more. Let the guards re-check their priming. Let the clerk stack one more armful of paper where the candle's pool leaned toward it. Let Madison fold resolution over resolution like dry kindling. Let fear search for the exit one more time and fail.

Another knock. Not frantic now. Single. Calm. The kind of knock that means *I already hold the key*.

The room breathed in.

The Sergeant's hand went to the bar and stayed there, pinned by his own tendons.

Paige set flint to steel and drew a slow, whispering spark. It drifted down onto the tar like a falling star and went out.

She drew another, and another; the third kissed the cord, brightened, and held. The flame was a kitten at first, uncertain on its feet. Then it liked the taste and grew teeth. It began to walk, slow, steady, curious, along the line she had laid, nosing into the shadow under the sideboard, finding cloth and oil and old dust, making friends.

Hancock smelled it before he saw it. His head jerked. "Do you—" he began, and then the first curl of smoke lifted by his elbow, polite as a question.

"Fire," someone said, no louder than a confession.

The Sergeant turned from the doors at last.

Paige settled back on her heels, eyes on the little orange animal she had let loose. Men rose in a rustle. A musket scraped; a chair tumbled; powder horns bumped and knocked.

She could have stood then and announced herself. It would have scratched the itch behind her teeth to tell them what they had already guessed. But the room was doing her speech for her. The cord glowed along the baseboard like a lit vein. The first flare under the sideboard whooshed, brief and hungry.

"Water!" Hancock barked, and two militiamen lurched toward a bucket that had never been filled.

Someone fired, not at the blaze, not at the gallery, at nothing. The shot deafened the nearest men and rattled the windows. A second shot answered it from the far wall, born of nothing but nerves. Sparks hopped from flint to spilled powder. The little orange animal showed its other face.

Paige watched the men see the trap and not yet understand who had set it, watched them understand only that they were many, and the exits were few, and the air was about to change.

She stood, at last, a shadow among shadows, invisible and entirely present.

Below, the doors boomed under the pressure of bodies pressing in, or out, or simply nearer to the story.

"Hold your fire!" Madison shouted, and his voice cracked into something human. He looked toward the gallery, toward the place where stories live, and in that instant Paige knew he had finally decided to believe in monsters.

~9
No Prosperity Left

Philadelphia woke to a sky the color of old bruises and a smell that wouldn't wash from the lungs, wet ash, cooked ink, pork fat, people. The Congress had eaten itself. The press had choked on a boy. Franklin had been peeled open by the storm he tried to leash. The city shuffled through the wreckage like a sleepwalker who'd torn up the house in a dream, looking at its hands and not recognizing what they'd done.

Women hosed the stoops with buckets, pushing congealed blood into the gutters where it swirled with horse piss and printer's ink. Boys gathered splintered beams, arguing which chunk had been a desk, which a door, which a man. Merchants pulled their shutters up halfway, then down again, listening for a shot that never came and swearing they had heard one anyway.

At the tavern, the one that now smelled more like meat than ale, the barmaid scrubbed a dark stain that kept coming back. The girl with the braid stood at the threshold, tankard in hand, staring into the street as if she could see the next hour coming and was trying to decide whether to meet it or hide. "We should leave," she said. "Before they count the bodies and do the math."

"Where would we go?" the widow asked. Her voice was gravel now, roughened by smoke and a scream she didn't remember giving. "The world belongs to men with pens and men with guns. We took the pens. The guns will come."

"They will," the barmaid said quietly. "But not yet."

Paige had slept against a wall in an alley that used to be a shortcut between two kinds of lies, a printer's door and a lawyer's stairs. She woke slick with soot, the quill stuck to her palm by dried blood. She peeled it free and rolled her stiff shoulders while the city talked to itself.

You did this.

We did this.

Someone did this.

There were preachers in the square by noon, hauling God out like a fire bucket. One shouted into the smoke that Satan wore a woman's face. Another promised bread for those who repented and rope for those who didn't. The crowd murmured in rhythm, hungry, superstitious, ready to be told who to blame and how hard.

Paige walked through them. Faces turned toward her and then away as if each person had been caught looking at a solar eclipse. A child pointed. His mother pinched his hand until he dropped it.

On Market Street, a man hammered a plank over a door and painted three words on it in hurried strokes: NO BUSINESS HERE. Underneath, in a smaller hand, someone had added: EVER AGAIN. A woman laughed when she saw it, then slapped her own mouth as if she'd said the wrong prayer out loud.

Down by the river, sailors gathered around a barrel fire and argued about ships, ports, destinations. "Charleston," a one-eyed man said. "Plague." "London," another said. "Rope." "Stay," the quietest of them said, staring at the water. "Burn." The river didn't care. It carried ash into the bay with the same patience it carried anything else.

Paige crossed the yard where a statue was supposed to be. The base was ready, pedestal smoothed, dates chiseled, but the figure had never gone up. The mason leaned against his cart, chewing a stolen apple to the core. "Man I never met," he said to nobody, holding his palm over the empty square where a bronze foot should have rested. "He was going to point at the horizon. Now he's pointing from the inside of a furnace." He tossed the apple into the hollow and walked away.

Above, the bells still rang for men who were gone. Half the city didn't know whether to cheer or kneel.

A column of militia turned the corner in uneven step, faces raw from the heat that had blossomed and died in the Congress. Their captain's voice rasped as he called halt—too many orders shouted over too little authority. They surrounded the blackened shell as if it might charge them. "Search parties," the captain told them, but his eyes flicked sideways at Paige before he remembered discipline and pretended not to see.

He had a list tucked into his cuff: names of women to question; taverns to overturn; alleys to sweep; a rumor about a child who had seen a woman with a quill and not been able to look away. He would die with that list in his hand, though he didn't know it yet.

Paige moved on.

She passed a church where the pews were stacked on the lawn, drying out. A girl not yet in her teens was chalking on the cobbles: a house, a pig, a woman with a knife bigger than her arm. The woman was smiling. The pig wore a judge's wig. When the chalk broke, the girl used the raw stub, determined, flattening the line into a smear that looked more like a wound than a drawing.

The girl saw Paige watching and drew a second woman next to the first, smaller, eyes wider, hair like a halo of furious scribbles. "That one's me," she said, so softly it almost wasn't voice. "Do I look like that?" She didn't blink while she waited for the verdict.

Paige didn't answer. She knelt, took the chalk, and added one more figure: a door drawn as an open mouth, black inside. The girl frowned at it. "Is it going to eat us?" she asked.

"If you step in," Paige said.

"If we don't?"

"It'll wait."

"Doors shouldn't wait," the girl said. "People wait."

Paige put the chalk back in the girl's hand and walked away.

By midafternoon, the square outside the ruins had become a marketplace of stories. A man swore he saw the witch fly. Another swore he saw her pray. A third insisted that when the Congress burned the air smelled like sugar, and the others told him to shut his mouth. None of them said the part they feared: that the fire had smelled like pork. The tongues of men are good at leaving things out.

A shriek cut the noise in half. Not terror, a hawker's pitch. A boy with a tray of paper scraps darted through the crowd. "News! News!" he cried, though the pages were blank. "Fresh news! News you can write yourself!" He sold out in minutes.

Paige watched a woman take one of the blank pages and tuck it into her dress. "For what?" a friend asked. "For later," the woman said, as if later were still a thing that could be planned for.

When the sun gave up and sank, the city exhaled. Lamps guttered to life in windows, each flame a tiny refusal. A night cart rattled down the lane collecting what the day had surrendered, broken chairs, charred beams, the wrong kind of memory. Its driver hummed the hymn they used at executions and funerals and weddings and any other occasion where the body was forced to stand still while the world moved.

Paige went back to the tavern.

The bodies were gone, hauled to the alley and stacked, then hauled from the alley when someone complained, then hauled back again when the someone who complained was found with a knife in his pocket and a liar's face on. The floor had been scrubbed until the boards were lighter than the rest of the room. You can tell where a thing has happened by where it is clean.

The barmaid was carving a potato with the concentration of a surgeon. The girl with the braid had a rope in her hands and was teaching her fingers a new knot. The widow mended a sleeve that belonged to nobody. The room had a quiet it hadn't had before not the quiet of exhaustion, but the quiet that follows a decision.

"You're late," the barmaid said without looking up.

Paige sat. "Busy day."

"Busy week," the widow said.

"Busy world," the girl added.

They ate what had not spoiled and drank what had, and for a long time nobody said the word *safe*. When someone finally did, it was a stranger at the door, hat in his hand, eyes on the floor. "Are we?" he asked, to the room or the air or the floorboards or his father's ghost. "Safe?"

"No," the barmaid said. "But we're together." She said it without romance, as if togetherness were a fact you could weigh on a scale and not a prayer.

The door banged open. Not militia, messengers, four of them, faces wind-burned, boots chewed to threads. They smelled of rain and news. One reached inside his coat and drew out a ribbon of parchment scorched at the edges. He slapped it on the bar. The ink had bled into itself, but the words were legible enough:

A Proclamation: By Authority of the Remainder of the Continental Congress. It said law would be restored. It said murderers would be found. It said witches would burn. It said property would be respected, especially the kind that could run. It said the nation would go on as if nations were boats you could patch with threats.

"Remainder," the widow said, tasting the word like a fruit and finding it full of worms.

The girl with the braid twisted the rope until it squealed. "Where are they?"

"Holed up in a customs house by the river," one messenger said. "Or in a cellar with a door that only opens one way," said another. "Or on a boat," said a third, and the fourth, who hadn't spoken, said nothing because there is always someone who knows the truth and knows better than to say it.

Paige read the proclamation without touching it. "They'll raid," she said. "Tonight, if they can. Tomorrow if they can't."

"Where?" the barmaid asked.

"Here," Paige said, and then, "Everywhere."

A bottle broke outside. Not a fight, a signal. The night changed temperature. There was a hum you could feel in your teeth.

The barmaid slid knives across the counter. The widow tucked her needle into her hair like a pin. The girl with the braid stood, the rope now a loop that knew what it wanted to be.

"Are we hiding?" the girl asked.

"No," Paige said.

"Running?"

"No."

"Begging?"

Paige almost smiled. "Never."

The tavern went black as the lamps were pinched shut. In the sudden dark they could hear boots finding stone, men finding formation, orders finding mouths. The city held its breath, not because it loved the people in the tavern but because it loved a story and knew this was the part where someone walked into an overwhelming light and someone else into an overwhelming dark.

Paige slid to the door and peered through the crack. A wedge of militia crowded the lane, muskets already at shoulder, eyes too bright. Not soldiers, exactly, fear with uniforms on. Behind them, neighbors stood at windows, faces smudged with smoke and doubt. Somewhere, a baby cried in the voice every baby uses when it knows the world is choosing sides again.

The captain raised his hand. "Open," he called. It wasn't a demand. It was a hope.

Nobody moved.

He tried again, louder. "By authority of—"

"Remainder," the widow said, just loud enough for the women to hear, and they almost laughed.

A boy in the line, a new recruit with a beard that hadn't decided what it wanted to be, swallowed hard and stared past Paige's face toward the dark tables behind her. His eyes slid away when she met them, then slid back as if curiosity and fear were playing tug-of-war with his neck.

Paige spoke through the crack, voice low, carrying. "You don't want to do this."

"We have orders," the captain said.

"You have a city," Paige said.

He hesitated. The men behind him shifted, the line wobbling in the way lines do when each man is trying to stand behind the man in front of him and there aren't enough fronts to go around.

"You will open," the captain said at last, and the attempt at iron in his voice bent in the middle.

Paige shut the crack and turned to the room. "Back," she said. Not retreat, just position. The barmaid slid behind the counter. The widow moved to the hearth. The girl with the braid crouched near the hinge where hands would reach first.

Outside, the captain lifted his hand again, but this time it wasn't for speech. The ram came forward: a beam with iron teeth. It kissed the door. The wood shivered.

"Three," Paige said.

"One," the beam whispered.

"Two."

"Two."

"___"

The door jumped in its frame.

Not yet, Paige told the room with her eyes.

Another blow. The bar split a little and remembered it had once been a tree and might break like one.

A third.

The latch groaned.

"Now," Paige said, and as the fourth blow came, she stepped aside and let the door in.

The tavern door was gone, splinters, smoke, a hole where order used to be. Paige stepped into the light of dawn, pistol in one hand, blade in the other. The street was a battlefield. Bodies in red and gray littered the cobblestones. The air stank of gunpowder, piss, and fear.

A handful of women still stood behind her, hair matted, dresses torn, faces streaked with soot and blood. The tavern itself belched smoke from its windows, a half-collapsed lung. Somewhere inside, the fire roared on, devouring what was left of the night.

The militia regrouped near the square, reloading by instinct more than reason. One man shouted for a line, another for God. None looked steady. Paige wiped a smear of blood from her cheek and started walking toward them.

They fired first. The crack of muskets shattered the morning calm. Splinters and glass rained from the tavern sign above her head. Paige didn't flinch. She raised her pistol and fired once. The lead shot punched through the officer's mouth, ripping the back of his head open. He dropped mid-command, and the rest scattered like dogs kicked from a carcass.

The women cheered, raw, ragged. Some screamed and charged, brandishing knives, broom handles, fireplace pokers. Paige let them. They had earned the rage.

The street turned to carnage. Men slipped on blood and mud. A woman leapt onto a soldier's back, driving a broken bottle into his throat. Another wrestled a bayonet away and plunged it through a chest plate. The sound of it, a crunch and a gasp, was almost human music.

When the smoke thinned, the women stood among the fallen.
Breathing hard.
Still alive.

Paige lowered her pistol. The barrel smoked like a candle snuffed too late.

From the church tower, the bell began to ring. Once, twice, then frantically, a signal. The alarm rolled across the city like thunder.

Paige turned to the tavern women.

"Leave," she said.

They stared back, unwilling. One asked, "And you?"

Paige reloaded. "They'll come again. Bigger this time."

The youngest shook her head. "Then we stay."

Paige looked at her, just a girl, maybe sixteen, blood spattered like freckles. "No," Paige said. "You tell what you saw. That's how this spreads."

The girl hesitated. "They'll call us witches."

Paige's mouth twitched. "Then you already know the words."

They scattered, fading into alleys and smoke. By the time the next regiment reached the square, Paige was gone.

~10
Fold to the Next Hunt

The city changed in less than a day. By noon, barricades had gone up around Congress Hall's ruins. Soldiers dragged corpses into carts. The stench of burned parchment hung heavier than death. Franklin's tower was a black tooth against the sky. Jefferson's house smoldered on the horizon.

Pamphlets still fluttered through the streets, half-burned declarations, scorched faces of "heroes." Children used them to start fires. One boy had tied a paper wig around his cat's neck. When the creature bolted through the square, people screamed. It looked too much like the ghosts they all expected.

Rumors fed on one another like rats. She was seen at the docks. She was seen at the graveyard. She was seen walking on water, blood still dripping from her hands.

The governor declared martial law before sunset. It didn't matter. The soldiers were too afraid to leave their posts after dark. Every alley looked like her.

Paige moved through the backstreets in silence. Her coat was burned at the edges. The pistol empty now. She didn't bother to reload. Every door she passed was bolted, but she could feel eyes behind them—watching, weighing, deciding whether to fear her or pray to her.

A rain began to fall, soft but steady. It hissed against the ash, turned blood into pink rivers along the gutters. The city breathed through its teeth. Somewhere, someone began to sing a hymn off-key, and it carried through the smoke like a ghost that didn't know it was dead.

Paige stopped under an awning where a printer's shop had stood. The sign still swung from a single nail. Inside, the press was a twisted skeleton of iron and wood. She touched it once, still warm. The smell of ink clung to her fingers.

Across the square, a crowd had gathered before a hanging notice.

REWARD: THE WOMAN WITCH.

Her likeness stared back from the paper, wrong hair, wrong jaw, but the eyes right enough to make people uneasy. Someone had drawn a halo above her head in charcoal. Another had slashed through it in red.

A woman spat on the poster. A man bowed his head. Two children stared until their mother yanked them away. Paige watched all of it. The city had already chosen its story; it just hadn't agreed on the ending.

She turned down Market Street, where shutters banged against the wind. The streets she'd first walked in silence now whispered her name. *The witch. The butcher. The saint.* No one called her Paige anymore. A wagon rolled past, piled high with bodies under tarps. Blood leaked through the wood and spattered the wheels. The driver didn't look up. He just cracked his whip and prayed under his breath.

As dusk neared, Paige reached the edge of the river. Smoke drifted low, thick as fog. The current dragged broken planks and the occasional limb out to sea. The sun dipped red behind the ruins of the bridge, light bending through smoke and mist, painting everything the color of rust.

On the far bank, a preacher shouted from the steps of a burned church. His voice cracked with conviction and madness. "The Lord remembers His chosen! He will strike the witch down!"

Paige didn't look at him. She crouched by the water, washing soot from her hands. The river turned pink where the blood bled out of her sleeves. She stared at her reflection—a flicker between woman and something else, the edges of her face wavering in the current.

The preacher's voice faltered. His flock had started to back away, whispering. She stood and turned to him, dripping water from her palms. The preacher froze mid-sentence, his words tangled in his throat.

Paige didn't smile. Didn't speak. She just looked. He dropped his Bible and ran. When she walked past the church steps, the book still lay open in the rain. The ink bled until every word became the same dark smear.

That night, the city burned in patches, little rebellions of fire where no one could stop them. The tavern women were gone, scattered or dead. The soldiers patrolled with torches, their shadows long and crooked on the walls. Inside a shuttered window, someone whispered prayers. Outside, someone else whispered her name like a secret that might save them.

Paige walked through it all, alone, the last figure moving in a city that didn't know if it had been saved or punished.

By dawn, the fires had gone out. The city didn't wake so much as exhale, like a corpse cooling after the last twitch.

Paige stood at the edge of the square where Congress had been. The marble columns were piles of white dust. The eagle emblems, the flags, the portraits, gone. Only the bronze bell had survived, cracked clean down the center, as if the sound itself had broken trying to escape.

The square was empty but for a few scavengers picking through debris. She watched one boy pry a gold button from a corpse's jacket. Another dragged a musket toward the docks, too heavy for his thin arms. The sun rose slow, gray and red through the haze, throwing long shadows over the ruin.

Paige didn't move until she saw her.

The freed girl from the auction stood across the square, barefoot, soot on her cheeks. She held something wrapped in cloth. When Paige crossed to her, the girl unwrapped it, a quill, blackened, the feather singed. Jefferson's.

"You dropped this," the girl said.

Paige stared at the object for a long moment. "No," she said softly. "It's yours now."

The girl frowned. "For what?"

"For when someone else forgets."

The girl nodded once, uncertain but solemn. Around them, the air shifted, quiet, heavy, like the pause before a storm or a verdict.

"You're leaving," the girl said.

Paige looked past her to the skyline, the burned steeples, the empty streets. "There's always another city," she said.

"Another man?"

Paige's jaw tightened. "Another lie."

The girl's eyes filled with something between anger and awe. "And who fixes what's left when you're gone?"

Paige almost smiled. "Maybe you."

She turned and started walking. The girl didn't follow. When Paige looked back once, she was gone, swallowed by the mist rising from the river. By the time she reached the outskirts, the smoke had thinned into a pale fog. The fields were still black with ash. The trees stood like charred ribs against the sky. Somewhere behind her, bells tolled, soft, uneven, more out of memory than faith.

Paige stopped on a hill overlooking what was left of Philadelphia. The city glowed faintly in the distance, scattered pockets of fire burning themselves out. She could see the river catching the light, red, gold, then black again.

For the first time since she arrived, she let herself breathe.

She had killed men who thought themselves gods, torn their words out by the roots, and left the ground bare. And yet the air already hummed with rebuilding, voices arguing, men reasserting order, history stitching itself back together like scar tissue.

It would always do that. That was its trick.

Paige crouched, dragging her fingers through the ash at her feet. It stuck to her skin, clinging like old ink. She thought of Jefferson's last breath, Adams's teeth scattering on the street, Franklin's body burning in his own lightning. Their words would fade now—letters unwriting themselves, faces softening in portraits—but something of them would remain, in the rot, in the language.

She couldn't kill it all. But she could keep cutting.

The air changed, pressure bending, the sound around her dimming, the light bending as if through water. She felt it before she saw it: the fold.

It wasn't a tear or a portal. It was absence made visible, the world forgetting itself, folding inward like a page turned too fast. The wind stilled. The ash rose in slow spirals. The colors drained until all that remained was her and the hum.

Somewhere inside it, whispers. Not voices she knew, but echoes of what came next. Fire. Screams. The crackle of torches. A woman crying out: *"Witch."*

Salem.

Paige took one last look at the city below. The ruins. The smoke. The silence.

She said, quietly, "Next."

Then she stepped forward, and the world closed over her like a flame going out.

About EATMS Productions

What's happening to women now is not random. It's structural.

Policy, culture, technology, and power are moving in the same direction.

EATMS maps them clearly and shows how to respond.

This title is part of an ongoing body of work. All EATMS Productions titles, across all series, authors, and formats, are components of a single connected project.

Start here: EATMS System Primer — Free Bundle
https://eatms.gumroad.com/l/dyvzbw

For full catalog or inquiries: eatms.me

Free survival booklet + EATMS updates: email "EATMS" to eatms@pm.me

Please feel free to burn part or all of this book, safely, as an effigy.

www.ingramcontent.com/pod-product-compliance
Lightning Source LLC
Chambersburg PA
CBHW030133260626
47156CB00008B/2930